The Impossible Medallion

♥ March 3, 2011 ♥

Dear Diary,

Hi! My name is Janie Ray and I am eleven years old. I got this diary for my birthday last month and promised my mom (her name is Sheila) that I would write in it if she bought it for me. I am in fifth grade, and believe it or not, my best friend is also named Sheila! Isn't that weird? She's really, really cool and we have tons of private jokes together. Like every time Mrs. Santini tells us to take out our math books, we totally crack up, because in the secret language we made up for our clubhouse, the letters m-a-t-h spell a really funny word. I'll tell you all about our language tomorrow.

Sheila has the best hair in our whole class and I am *so* jealous! She always complains about her hair, but I think she's crazy. It's long and straight and never sticks out. She thinks it's boring, but I would do *anything* to trade with her! My hair is incredibly thick and frizzy, and I usually wear it in a ponytail, because otherwise my mom says it's too messy.

Sheila has a huge crush on Calvin, who sits behind her in class. He's really cute. I think he likes her too, but she doesn't believe me, and she won't even sit next to him at lunch time.

I don't have a crush on anyone. I mean, I don't think boys are gross, but personally, I don't see why we have to get all googly eyed about them.

Oh my gosh, I have a huge math test tomorrow (m-a-t-h!!), so I have to go now. I did really badly on my last test, and my mom will be so mad if I don't study for this one.

Dear Diary,

URGH! I had my math test today, and it was horrible! We'll get our grades back next week, but I compared answers afterwards with Sheila, and I think I got at least three questions wrong. I seriously don't understand why we need to learn math. My dad (his name is Mark) says it will help me later on in life, but personally, I don't see why. I mean, it's not like I'm planning to be a mathematician or anything!

The rest of the day was pretty boring. At lunch, Marcia the Snob grabbed the piece of paper Sheila was doodling on and almost found out about her crush on Calvin! Sheila had drawn lots of little hearts with arrows through them and written "Sheila and Calvin" all over in pink magic marker. Lucky for her, she wrote it in our secret language, so MTS (Marcia the Snob, of course) had no idea what it said. That didn't stop her from jumping up and down, waving the paper around like a crazy person, and screeching, "Ooh, it looks like Sheila has a crush on *somebody!*" That MTS is such a pain!

Oh, I almost forgot! I promised to tell you about our secret language today. So here is the code (you just have to switch each letter of the alphabet with the secret letter underneath it):

A	B	C	D	E	F	G	H	I	J
o	h	r	m	i	q	n	k	e	p
K	**L**	**M**	**N**	**O**	**P**	**Q**	**R**	**S**	**T**
g	d	t	s	u	w	v	z	l	j
U	**V**	**W**	**X**	**Y**	**Z**				
a	x	f	b	y	c				

My name in code is "POSEI" and Sheila's is "LKIEDO". So instead of Sheila and Calvin, her note said "LKIEDO OSM RODXES".

TJL EL O WOES!!!!

(Oh, and in case you haven't figured it out yet, m-a-t-h spells DUMB! Coincidence? I think not.)

♥ March 8, 2011 ♥

Dear Diary,

Today was the worst. The absolute pits.

It started out o.k. – I got up on time to have breakfast and even made it to school a few minutes early. It always makes my mom very happy when I have breakfast. She says it's the most important meal of the day and loves making us pancakes and French toast and stuff, even though she only ever has coffee herself.

I think parents like to see their kids eat. I don't really get it, though. They seem to spend all their time trying to get us to eat *more*, while they're busy trying to eat *less* themselves. Every time we have a big meal, my dad complains that he ate too much and my mom unbuttons her pants and says she feels "fat". But if we don't eat everything on *our* plates, they tell us we should finish up so that we can join the "Clean Plate Club". When I was little, I actually thought there was a club like that, and that if I ate all my food I would get to join.

Go figure. Grown-ups sure are weird sometimes.

The first couple of hours at school weren't too bad, either. During English class, I got to switch seats with Jessica. Mrs. Santini made her move, because she couldn't stop talking to her friend Alexis. And I'm really happy about it, since it means I don't have to sit next to Ben White anymore. Ben *really* gets on my nerves. He always puts his elbows on my side of the table, and when I ask him to move over, he just grunts and moves like one inch. He's the kind of kid who brings five sharpened pencils to every test, even though he never breaks any of them. And he always knows the answers in math class. Once my pencil broke during a history test, and there he was, with all those pencils laid out on the desk next to him. But would he let me borrow one? No! Isn't that just the most obnoxious thing ever?? No offense, but that is such a *boy* thing to do.

Anyway, I got to move and sit next to Alexis. She's a pretty nice kid, even though she's friends with MTS. She has this thing about Angry Birds, and all her things – her notebooks, her pencil case, and even her erasers – are covered with them. Go figure. And she's really into sports. Her mom always packs her amazing lunches, with stuff I would never be allowed to have – like peanut butter and Marshmallow Fluff sandwiches – and she's usually willing to share her food with people.

Anyway, it was after that that everything started going downhill. First, MTS and her friends all started giggling when they saw me in the hallway during recess. I have no idea why. They are such banana brains! Then, in math class, I got my test back and got a lousy 78. I think Sheila did better than me, but I'm not really sure, because she never tells anyone her grades. Her mom says grades are private. In general, though, she does pretty well in school.

At lunch, I tripped on my shoelaces and dropped my tray all over the floor, and some of my pudding landed on Calvin's shoes! He was really nice about it, but Sheila said she almost died.

But the most horrible part was when I got home in the afternoon. I caught SRJ (Silly RJ, of course) in my room, playing with my (new, amazing, totally-off-limits-to-RJ) tablet! I shrieked at the top of my lungs, and my mom came rushing in to see what happened. But of course, instead of yelling at SRJ, she yelled at *me* and told me I was setting a bad example for him. A bad example!? He was the one cackling like a wild hyena just to make me mad. SRJ *always* goes into my room and touches my stuff, and my parents never get mad at him, because they say he's only four years old and doesn't know any better. It's so unfair! When I was four, they never let *me* get away with anything. I had to clean my room practically every day, and his room is always a huge mess. I'm officially not speaking to my mom.

♥ March 9, 2011 ♥

Dear Diary,

Turns out yesterday was only the *second* worst day of my life. When I got to school this morning, I found out what MTS and her dumb friends had been giggling about. As soon as I walked into the classroom, everyone suddenly got quiet, and I saw a huge picture of a lion taped to the front of my desk with the words "JANIE the FRIZZ" scribbled underneath! MTS and her lousy gang were all standing by the blackboard, covering their mouths with their hands and looking at the floor, and I just knew they had something to do with it. I ran out of the room and hid in the bathroom crying, until Sheila came looking for me after first recess (she had a dentist's appointment this morning). I've never been so humiliated in my entire life!

All day long, people roared at me and made stupid lion comments when they saw me in the hall. Why does MTS have to be so mean? What did I ever do to her?

The worst part is, I think MTS must have overheard my mom reminding me at drop off the other day to wear my scrunchie, so that my hair wouldn't frizz! Now I'm doubly not speaking to my mom. She always looks so nice and everything is always so easy for her! I'll bet *she* never got made fun of at school.

♥ March 12, 2011 ♥

Dear Diary,

Today is Saturday and it's raining out. Sheila and I were supposed to go play kickball in the park this morning, but the field is all muddy and the game was cancelled.

Things with my mom are really weird. At breakfast this morning she made us pancakes with chocolate chips *and* French toast, and she even gave me hot apple cider with a cinnamon stick. I didn't tell her about what happened at school last week, but I guess she can tell I'm pretty mad about *something*. I tried to keep up not speaking to her, but by the end of breakfast I kind of laughed at some of her jokes and let her give me a hug. But I'm still mad!

She told me that when she was my age, she used to get angry at *her* mom for taking her sister's side and yelling at her when they fought. I'm not sure I believe her, though. I can't even imagine my mom fighting with Auntie Karen. I'll bet she was Little Miss Perfect when she was eleven!

♥ March 13, 2011 ♥

Dear Diary,

You are seriously not going to believe what happened to me this morning. I was cleaning my room and came across this old medallion I found when I was seven, on our vacation in Miami. It's really neat – shiny, black, round and smooth - and it has a really weird inscription on it:

Posei: Kudm jenkjdy osm loy jki moji a fosj ju xelej jkzii jetil

It's been sitting in my jewelry box for years, and when I saw it yesterday, I suddenly noticed something incredible: *The first word of the inscription, which never made any sense to me, spells my name in the secret language I made up with Sheila!*

That got me thinking, and I decided to see what would happen if I plugged our code into the rest of the inscription, just for the heck of it. And this is the unbelievable part, the part that doesn't make any sense. Turns out the inscription says:

Janie: hold tightly and say the date u want to visit three times

If I hadn't seen that medallion and its crazy inscription with my own two eyes, years before Sheila and I ever even made up our code, I'd figure it was MTS trying to play some kind of a trick on me or something. So I don't blame you if you think I'm nuts. I would too, if I were you. It's impossible!!!

Naturally, I called Sheila right away, and she nearly choked on her cucumber sticks when she saw it. Luckily, she's seen the medallion before, so she knows I'm not making it up.

"Hold tightly and say the date you want to visit three times"? What in heck could that mean? How could something have been written in our secret language *four years* before we even made it up? And how in the world am I supposed to concentrate on my English homework tonight?

Sheila and I are having a special meeting in our clubhouse tomorrow after school to talk about this mystery and try and figure things out. Meanwhile, I gotta go — my mom wants me to come down for dinner, and I have to hide the medallion so that SRJ doesn't find it.

♥ March 14, 2011 ♥

Dear Diary,

If you thought I was nuts yesterday, you're really going to freak out today. This whole medallion thing keeps getting weirder and weirder!

This morning I could barely concentrate on anything at school, even in English class. Mrs. Moore called on me three times and yelled at me for not knowing what page they were on. On the bright side, I nearly forgot about the whole lion business, and it seems like most of the kids in the class have forgotten about it too. Except for MTS & Company, that is.

Right after school, Sheila and I ran home as fast as we could, grabbed a snack and went out to the clubhouse to talk about *the situation*. What happened next took us both by surprise, and even though it's still today (or at least, I hope it is), so much has happened, and I'll just have to tell you the story…

******

"I don't know, Janie," Sheila said uncertainly, bouncing a rubber ball against the clubhouse wall. "There has to be a reasonable explanation for this. Maybe this is a *different* medallion than the one you found when you were seven. Maybe MTS or someone figured out how to switch the medallion you had with a new one. Nothing else makes any sense!"

"I know," I answered. "But first of all, MTS doesn't even know our language, and she's never been in my room! And second, I specifically remember the medallion having a strange inscription on it when I found it."

"Well," she said, thoughtfully chewing a hangnail off her pinky. "I've always wondered how I would react if something unbelievable happened. Like if someone had special powers or something and managed to prove they could lift things with their eyes or read people's thoughts. I've always wondered whether I'd believe them or not, or whether I'd be too scared to accept the possibility that things we don't believe in might actually be true. This is kind of like that, right?"

"What do you mean?"

"Well, here we have a situation where something seemingly impossible has happened, and we can't explain it any other way. I don't know, maybe we should just accept that something unusual really *is* going on."

"Ok," I said, picking up the medallion and turning it over in my hands. "Let's say we *do* accept that we don't know what's going on. What should we do?"

There was quiet as we each considered my words.

"Well," Sheila finally said, grinning mischievously. "Maybe we should just do what it says."

"Huh?" I said, startled.

"Maybe we should do what it says," Sheila repeated quietly. "Hold it tightly and say the date we want to visit three times."

"What, you mean – time travel?" My eyes widened.

"I guess," she answered. "Or at least, I think that's what I mean."

"Well, where should we go?" I asked. "Or rather, *when* should we go?

We both giggled excitedly. Sheila wrinkled her brow before suddenly grabbing my hand, grasping it together with the medallion, and blurting out, "July 5, 1739! July 5, 1739! July 5, 1739!"

******

Holy cow. Geez Louis. Yikes!!!

After Sheila grabbed my hand, everything went haywire. We plunged down into a dark tunnel and fell, shrieking our heads off, for what seemed like forever. It was kind of like being in an elevator that's going down super fast, making you feel like your tummy is about to fly up into your nose and your head is going to explode.

Then we landed with a *thump* in a small, rocky clearing, surrounded by trees as far as the eye could see.

Sheila got up first, brushed herself off, and looked around. "Where the heck are we?"

I rubbed my eyes and stood up slowly. "I don't know," I said quietly, trying not to panic. My trembling voice was drowned out by a loud noise behind me, and I whirled around to see a huge pine tree swaying back and forth and looking like it was about to fall over.

"Watch out!" I yelled, shoving Sheila out of the way. I pushed her onto the ground and landed in a heap on top of her.

"Hey, what are you-" she started to protest. But then she grew silent, a stunned look on her face, as the humongous tree toppled over and crashed about two feet away from us. It was so big that it made the ground shake.

We sat there speechless for several seconds, and I pinched myself to make sure I wasn't dreaming. *This seriously could **not** be happening.*

I turned to Sheila and opened my mouth to speak, but before I could say anything, I saw something out of the corner of my eye that shocked me back into silence. A huge man with really strange clothes was walking towards us, looking very angry.

And worst of all, he was carrying an axe!

"Who is there?" he thundered. He was speaking English, but I couldn't place his accent. As he got nearer, I could see he looked about my dad's age, and his face – which was kindly, despite his anger - took on a concerned expression. "What are you two girls doing on my property? And why are you unattended! Are you hurt? I am chopping wood here today! And I am sure I do not have to tell you how perilous that can be!" He peered down at us and furrowed his brow. "What are you girls wearing? Where are you from?"

Sheila and I glanced at each other, and then, as if by unspoken agreement, we both scrambled to our feet and started running away as fast as we could. We must have taken the man by surprise, because he just stood there, his mouth open, and watched us go.

We ran and ran for what seemed like hours, but was probably more like ten minutes, before Sheila stopped and leaned against a tree.

"Wait," she said between breaths. "I need my inhaler." Sheila has asthma, and always carries a small, white inhaler with her in her pocket.

"Ok." I looked around, catching my breath, and was relieved to see no one had followed us. We were in the middle of a forest, with pine trees all around, and in the distance I could hear the faint sound of running water. A creek? I reached up to brush a few stray strands of hair out of my eyes. My head was hot and sweaty, and my hair felt even frizzier than usual. It must have been close to ninety degrees out! *Not March weather at all,* I thought. I pinched myself again, wondering if maybe I was just losing my mind.

"Wow." Sheila broke into my thoughts. "T-t-this is u-unbelievable! D-do you think we really t-travelled through time?" She had an awed look on her face as she stuffed the inhaler back in her pocket.

"I don't know…" My voice trailed off.

"Well, t-that guy sure didn't look like he lived in the twenty-first century." Sheila managed a weak smile.

I nodded mutely. That was for sure.

"So what should we do now?" Sheila moved a couple of rocks out of her way and sat down on the ground, suddenly all business. "Let's make a plan. You still have the medallion, right?"

That's one great thing about Sheila - she can be pretty impulsive sometimes, but she's a very practical person.

My heart skipped a beat, and I reached into my pocket, breathing a sigh of relief when I felt the cool medallion against the palm of my hand. "Yup, it's here." I sat down next to her.

"Ok, so the way I see it, we have two options. We can stay here and explore a bit or -"

I shook my head vigorously. "No way. We need to get out of here right away! We don't even know where - or when! - we are!"

Sheila giggled. "Sure we do! We're in 1739."

I shook my head again. "Just because you said 1739, that doesn't mean that's where we are. We don't even know how this medallion works! Then I stopped. "Wait a minute. Why did you choose 1739, anyway?"

Sheila giggled again. "I don't know, I just thought it would be cool to see all that stuff we're learning about in history class. Like the Boston Tea Party."

I rolled my eyes. Sheila might be better than me in math, but history was my favorite subject. "The Boston Tea Party happened in 1773, genius. We just learned about that two days ago! And anyway, it happened in *Boston*." I gestured to the trees around us. "We could be in Timbuktu for all we know."

Sheila gave me a sheepish smile. "Well, I was close," she said.

Just then I heard another loud noise coming from behind Sheila, and looked up to see a horse galloping in our direction.

"Watch out!" I yelled for the second time at the top of my lungs, rolling aside and pulling Sheila with me. I buried my face in my hands and waited for the horse to go by, praying it wouldn't trample us.

A few seconds passed, and I heard a loud whinnying. Then someone said "Whoa boy!" and the galloping came to a slow halt. When I finally picked up my head, I saw a young girl, about our age, standing over us with her hands on her hips. She was short and thin, and was wearing a dark brown dress with what looked like a white apron over it. Her hair was pulled back into a neat braid, partially covered with a gleaming white bonnet, but her dress was incredibly dirty and one of her sleeves had a big hole in it.

"Who are you?" she demanded, shifting her weight from one side to the other. Her horse, which she had already managed to tie to a nearby tree, whinnied loudly again. "Quiet!" she said, swatting it with a small stick she picked up from the ground.

Sheila and I just sat there, and I opened my mouth, but the words were stuck in my throat.

"I said, who are you?" she demanded again. Then her eyes narrowed. "Are you boys or girls?"

That seemed to break the spell, and Sheila jumped up and faced the girl indignantly. "Hey, what is that supposed to mean?"

The girl took a step back, surprised, and stared at us for several moments. "I apologize," she said finally. "I can see you are girls. But I have never seen girls wearing pants before! And I am not sure what hay has to do with anything!" Then she grinned and gestured to the horse. "I like girls who are not afraid to do what boys do. My parents hate it when I ride George. They say a *little lady* like me should not go horseback riding alone." She said the words *little lady* in a mimicking tone, and then wrinkled her nose and snorted. "But I think they are just old fashioned!" She stuck out her hand. "My name is Penelope. What are your names?"

Sheila reached out and shook her hand. "My name is Sheila!" she said. "And this is Janie." She helped me up and I stood slowly, brushing the pine needles off my jeans.

"Nice to meet you!" Penelope said. "Where are you from? You do not look like you are from here."

Sheila and I met each other's eyes. "No, we aren't from here. We're kind of - lost." I managed.

The girl gave me a funny look. "You have an odd way of speaking," she said. "Well, maybe I can help you find your way. Where are you trying to go?"

"Boston!" Sheila blurted out, before I had a chance to reply. I shot her a look.

The girl's eyes widened. "Boston? That is almost 700 miles away from here! Even if you had a horse and carriage, it would take you more than two weeks to get there!"

"Uh, where are we?" I asked. I didn't dare ask her *when* we were. She already thought we were complete lunatics.

The girl looked at me strangely again. "We are in Edenton, North Carolina, of course." *Edenton, North Carolina?!* A chill went down my spine.

Then she pointed off in the distance. "I live over there. I cannot take you to Boston, but I am certain my parents would not mind having guests for supper. They are going to be furious when they see what I have done to my dress." She pointed at the hole in her sleeve and winked at us. "But they may not scold me as much if there is company. My house is just one mile away. You will come with me."

It was a statement, not a question. I looked at Sheila and was surprised to see her nodding eagerly.

"Uh, that's very kind of you," I said to Penelope. "I just need to talk to my friend in private for a minute." I grabbed Sheila's elbow and pulled her aside.

Penelope sniffed. "Do you not know it is rude to share secrets when others are around?" She turned and started walking slowly towards her horse, shaking her head. "I will wait for you over here."

As she walked away, I turned to face Sheila. "Are you insane?" I whispered. "We can't go with her. We have to get out of here!"

"Why?" Sheila asked, and I could tell by the gleam in her eye that it was no use trying to convince her. "We have the medallion. If anything happens, we can just use it to go home." She put her hand on my shoulder. "Please, Janie? Just think how much fun it'll be! And what if we really are in 1739? That would be the coolest thing EVER!"

I took a deep breath. She did have a point. If we could use the medallion to get home, there would be no harm in waiting a little while and exploring a bit. And if we were going to stay here, going to Penelope's house made more sense than trying to find our way all alone in the forest. Especially since we didn't have water or food or anything. At the thought of food, my stomach growled, and it occurred to me I hadn't eaten anything but a little snack since lunchtime. I reached into my pocket and fingered the medallion. "Ok," I said finally. "Let's go - but only for a short time!"

Sheila gave me a quick hug and squealed with excitement. "This is going to be EPIC!!"

*****

We followed Penelope in the direction of her house, silently trudging through the forest. Except for the sound of branches and leaves crackling under our feet, and a few birds chirping in the distance, everything seemed oddly quiet. I nudged Sheila in the ribs and whispered in her ear, "Do you hear that?"

"Hear what?"

"Exactly. There are no cars or trucks or anything!"

Sheila stopped and listened for a few seconds before nodding. "Yeah, it's pretty creepy."

We continued walking in an awkward silence for another twenty minutes or so, before arriving at a small, two-story white house with wooden panels and a large yard closed off by a yellow fence. "This is my house!" Penelope said proudly, tying her horse to a tree. Then she faced us, lowering her voice and speaking quickly. "There is an elderly woman who lives in our town and keeps to herself. Her name is Emily Hodgson. If my parents ask you where you are from, tell them that she is your grandmother, and that you are visiting her for the summer from Virginia. They never speak to her, so they will not discover the truth. And do not tell them your real names." She pointed at Sheila. "You will be Patience." Then she pointed at me.

"And you will be Modesty."

Sheila stifled a giggle, and I frowned. It would so *figure* that I would get the really weird name.

"Um, ok." I said, brushing away the uneasy feeling that was starting to form in the pit of my stomach. *And what if they didn't believe us?*

"No, wait a minute." Penelope was looking us up and down and shaking her head. "This will not do at all. Your clothes are too odd, and my parents will be suspicious. Wait here."

Before we could protest, she raced to the side of the house and started climbing up a large oak tree that was almost touching an upstairs window. She opened it and tumbled inside, emerging a few seconds later with something wrapped around her shoulders.

"She's quite the little lady," Sheila said with a wry grin. I smiled in spite of myself.

Penelope ran back in our direction and shoved two dresses with matching bonnets at us. "Go behind that tree and put these on. I shall hide your things."

We did what she said, and I breathed a sigh of relief when the dress slid easily onto me. I was at least two sizes taller than Penelope, but the dress seemed to be a one-size-fits-all kind of thing, with strings you could pull to adjust the width. It was a little short on me, but not too bad.

As Penelope opened the door to her house, a tall, plump woman with a tight, graying bun in her hair walked up and took her by the arm. She looked pretty mad. "Penelope Padgett! Why, I never saw a young lady as filthy as you are today! Go right upstairs and -" She stopped abruptly and stared us. "Who -"

"These are my new friends, Mamma! Patience and Modesty," Penelope said quickly. "They are visiting their grandmother from Virginia and I would like to invite them to join us for supper!"

The woman stood up straight and eyed us suspiciously. I kicked myself. I should have taken off my scrunchie! They probably didn't have *those* in 1739. We must have passed some kind of a test though, because her face softened. "Of course they may stay," she said to Penelope. "But you *must* go upstairs and change your clothes. I hope you were not riding that awful horse again!"

"Ok, Mamma." Penelope muttered. "Come, girls, you may wait with me in my room."

I glanced around as we climbed up the stairs, taking in our surroundings. The house definitely looked old-fashioned, and it suddenly struck me that there were no light switches on any of the walls. The wooden floor was bare, with no carpeting, and the paint on the walls was peeling.

But it was as we followed Penelope down a long hallway to her room, that I saw something that nearly knocked my socks off. On a small decorative table that stood by her door lay a newspaper called the "South Carolina Gazette". And under the name of the paper, in unmistakable print, was the date: July 5th, 1739. I shivered and wrapped my arms around my chest. *This doesn't make any sense,* I thought, putting my hand on the table to steady myself as a wave of dizziness washed over me. *People don't just travel through time!*

Penelope's room didn't look that much different from the rest of the house. There was a simple single bed in the corner, a small closet, and a place for candles. Several pieces of clothing were strewn about on the floor. I nudged Sheila. "I guess she doesn't have a TV in her room, huh."

Sheila giggled softly. "I guess not."

Penelope gestured for us to sit down on her bed and began pulling off her dress without even asking us to look away. I tried not to stare, but I couldn't help stealing curious glances, and it soon became clear why she didn't mind changing in front of two perfect strangers - she was wearing more clothes under her dress than most people wear at all! She threw the dirty dress on the floor and rummaged around in her closet for a clean one.

Sheila tapped me on the shoulder and winked. "I didn't know they had messy rooms in the olden days," she whispered.

"What?" Penelope said, looking at Sheila with a furrowed brow. "What did you say?"

"Oh - I, uh, just," Sheila stammered. "I was just telling Janie that I also have a messy room."

"Messy? Oh, you mean disorderly." Penelope smiled. "Yes, my mother always wants me to put everything away just so, but I cannot be bothered. She spends all her time cleaning the house, and never does anything fun!"

My eyes wandered to the window, and I saw two girls sitting outside, weaving something on a large loom, like the ones I had seen when I visited Colonial Williamsburg with my parents last year. It looked like something out of a movie set.

Penelope must have noticed me staring, because then she said, "Those are my two sisters, Elizabeth and Sarah. Do you have any brothers or sisters?"

"Yeah, I have a little brother," I said. "He's kind of a pain."

"A pain?" Penelope furrowed her brow again. "You mean he is ill?"

I winced. "No, I just mean - He can be a little bit annoying sometimes."

Penelope looked relieved. "Yes, I know what you mean. My older sister

Elizabeth is such a goody two-shoes! She always does exactly what Mamma tells her, and she dresses nicely every day. My sisters share a room, and it is always in perfect order! Sometimes I cannot stand them."

Then I had an idea. "Hey, would it be ok if I took a look at the newspaper on the table over there?" I asked.

"What?" Penelope turned to look at me, both eyebrows raised. "You mean the South Carolina Gazette? You know how to read?"

"I, um, I -" I stuttered and looked helplessly at Sheila. *What was the right answer?*

"Yes, our fathers taught us both to read," Sheila rescued me. "They, um, think it is important for girls to get an education."

Penelope sighed and walked over to the door, returning with the newspaper. "You are very lucky. I have been trying to teach myself to read these past few months, but it is still very hard for me."

"You mean, you don't have to go to school?" I asked.

She shook her head. "No, there is no school in this area."

Just then we heard a harried voice calling from downstairs, "Penelope! It is almost time for supper! Please set the table right away! Why must I ask you again?"

"Ok, Mamma!" Penelope called back. She motioned for us to follow her. "Come, it is time to eat."

After Penelope left the room, Sheila quickly ripped off the front page of the paper and stuffed it into her apron pocket. I raised my eyebrows at her, and she grinned. "Just a little souvenir. You know, for history class."

*****

We helped Penelope set the table with large wooden plates and spoons, and as I was putting the last plate down on the table, the door opened and a tall man walked in. When I saw his face, my blood ran cold and I grabbed Sheila by the arm.

"Ouch!" she said, pulling away from me.

"It's him!" I whispered.

"What?"

"Don't look now, but the man who just came in is the guy with the axe! I guess he must be her father!"

Sheila looked up automatically and gasped.

"I said, don't look!"

"Well, what should we do?" Sheila's forehead was creased with worry.

"I don't know. Maybe we should go back home now." I reached for my pocket and nearly fainted as my hand felt the stiff fabric of the dress Penelope had given me. *I wasn't wearing my own clothes anymore, and the medallion was still in my jeans pocket!!* My mouth went dry and I swallowed hard, trying desperately to think back to what Penelope had said when she gave us the clothes.

Where had she said she had hidden our stuff?

Keeping my face turned to the side, I came up behind Penelope and asked quietly, "Um, where did you put my clothes?" I tried to keep my voice nonchalant.

Penelope smiled. "Do not worry, your things are in a safe place. I will show you later."

I hesitated. If I pressed her, she might get suspicious and want to see for herself why I needed my clothes so badly. But how long could we keep this up without her dad realizing that we were the strange kids he had seen in the forest?

I pulled Sheila into the next room and explained the situation. "I don't think we have a choice. We'll have to wait until after supper to get the medallion back. And maybe he won't recognize us. He only saw us for a few seconds, and we were wearing different clothes!"

We walked back into the kitchen, where the family had already begun assembling around the table. The man had taken his place at the head of the table, and Penelope's mom was sitting across from him at the other end. Penelope motioned for us to sit down next to her.

"Modesty, perhaps you would like to say grace?" Penelope's father had an expectant look on his face, and it took me a few seconds to realize he was talking to me.

"Um, I -" *Now what?*

The family was holding hands around the table, so I took Penelope and Sheila's hands in mine and squeezed them, trying to conjure up the blessings I had learned in Sunday school. Finally I managed, "Um, Thank you, Lord, for this food and, um, bless the hands that prepared it."

That seemed to do the trick, because they all answered "Amen", picked up their spoons and began to eat. Sheila caught my eye and winked at me. "Way to go!" she mouthed silently.

I took a tentative bite of the pudding and bread Penelope's mom put on the table, mentally preparing myself to just chew and swallow, no matter how bad it was. I'm not the pickiest eater in the world - at least not compared to RJ - but I'm not one of those kids that likes everything, either. Hmm. It was actually kind of good! I heard loud slurping noises next to me and cast a glance at Sheila, who was busy gulping down her food, attracting strange looks from Penelope's sisters.

"So, where are you girls from?" Penelope's father had put his spoon down and was eyeing us strangely.

"Um, we're from Virginia," Sheila replied. "We're here visiting our grandmother, Emily Hodgson."

Wow, she was good.

"Emily Hodgson? I did not know she had grandchildren." Penelope's father looked thoughtful. "She is such a quiet and strange old woman. You know," he added after a pause, "many people have wondered whether she is a witch."

"Samuel!" Penelope's mother chided him. "What a terrible thing to say. I am quite certain that their grandmother is a perfectly nice lady!" She turned to us. "Where are you from in Virginia, dears?"

Where in Virginia? "Um, Williamsburg?" I said. That was the first place that popped into my mind. I crossed my fingers, hoping they didn't know too many people there.

"Ah, Williamsburg is a fine place." Penelope's father let out a large belch. "Elizabeth, dear, you have prepared a wonderful supper. Now I must go, I have patients to attend to." He stood up and left the table, patting his eldest daughter on the head.

Penelope stood up too. "I shall take my friends back to their grandmother's house now," she said, motioning for us to follow.

"Thank you so much for a delicious meal," Sheila said, pushing her chair back and standing up.

"Yes, we are, uh, very grateful for your kindness," I added. It was funny how we were starting to talk so formally after being there for just a couple of hours.

Once outside, Penelope led us through a grassy field and into a small barn that looked like it was falling apart. The sun was setting, and it was already getting dark. "You shall sleep here," she pronounced. "And in the morning we will make a plan to get you back home." She seemed to have assumed we were actually *from* Boston, and I certainly wasn't about to correct her.

"Um, ok… But Penelope, where are our things?" I made a huge effort to keep the panic out of my voice.

She rolled her eyes. "I told you already that you do not need to worry. I have put them in a safe place, and I will give them back to you in the morning. It is better that they remain hidden until you leave."

Sheila and I exchanged worried glances. How had we let this happen? We were at this girl's mercy now, and we just had to pray she didn't go through our stuff or try and keep us here.

"Now go to sleep," she said firmly, walking towards the door of the barn. "I will come and wake you before dawn. Good night!"

As the door swung shut behind Penelope, Sheila and I slumped down on the piles of hay we were supposed to sleep on and I scowled at her.

"What?" she said, defensively.

"If you hadn't insisted on staying here, we wouldn't be in this mess. Who knows what she's gonna do with our stuff! We might be stuck here forever!" I lay down on my back and closed my eyes.

Sheila just sat there, pushing hay around with her foot and chewing glumly on a fingernail. "I'm sorry," she said quietly. "You're right."

Somehow, hearing her admit she was wrong didn't feel quite as good as I thought it would. I sat up and put my hand on her shoulder. "Well, I guess it's not really your fault. I agreed to stay too! And I'm the one who left the medallion in my stupid jeans pocket."

Sheila smiled at me gratefully. "Whoever's fault it is, we have to get our stuff back and get the heck out of here! I say we get a few hours' sleep, and then as soon as Penelope wakes us in the morning, we grab our clothes and make a run for it."

"Sounds like a plan."

******

My eyes started to close the moment my head hit the pile of hay I was using for a pillow, and the next thing I knew, I awoke with a start. I could have sworn it was just a few minutes later, but a faint light had already begun peeking in through the cracks in the barn. I rubbed my eyes, reached over and tapped Sheila on the shoulder. "Um, do you have any idea what they do around here for bathrooms?"

Sheila grunted and turned over, pulling the thin blanket we had been using over her head. "No idea," she mumbled. "Maybe you should just find a tree or something."

Ugh. Have I mentioned I *hate* going to the bathroom in nature?

I rolled off the pile of hay and quietly tiptoed outside, looking for a place to do my business. And that's when I heard the footsteps. Someone was coming! I slipped behind the nearest tree and craned my neck to listen, my heart racing. I heard the creak of the barn door swinging open and then a female voice that sounded like Penelope's mother:

"Where are you really from?"

There was a muffled reply, and then what sounded like a male voice:

"It was only after I fell asleep that I realized that you are the girls I saw in the forest yesterday, wearing those strange clothes. Emily Hodgson is not really your grandmother, is she? We shall pay Mrs. Hodgson a visit, right now! Where is your sister? If that is really what she is!"

I held my breath, frantically going over my options in my mind. *Calm down, Janie,* I told myself, *think!* I could run out and join Sheila, who was probably terrified, but then what about the medallion? There had to be a way to -

The footsteps were getting closer again, and I heard Sheila say loudly, "She's not here! She went home to our grandma's house!" It seemed like Sheila was trying to send me a message, and I suddenly realized what I had to do.

I waited until the footsteps had faded and took a few tentative steps out from behind the tree. In the distance, I could see Penelope's parents getting into a carriage with Sheila and I ran as fast as I could to the front door of the house. I tried the handle, and a knot formed in the pit of my stomach when it wouldn't turn.

Of course it wouldn't. It was locked.

I turned and ran around to the side of the house, and when I reached the big oak tree outside Penelope's window, I stopped and took in several deep breaths. Let's just say climbing trees is not exactly my *favorite* thing in the world. It's not that I'm afraid of heights. It's more like - I'm afraid of falling.

I closed my eyes and grabbed the first branch. It was surprisingly easy to pull myself up, and just a few seconds later I was outside Penelope's window. *Whatever you do, don't look down*, I told myself firmly. The window was just a few inches from the tree, but my heart stopped as I reached out and held onto the window sill. Luckily, the window was open halfway and there was enough room for me to jump through it. I counted to ten.

Here goes nothing.

I landed hard on Penelope's floor and picked myself up, stifling a yelp as I stubbed my toe on the side of her bed. She was snoring softly, not a care in the world, and I felt like throttling her.

"Penelope, wake up!" I whispered urgently. When she didn't respond, I reached out and shook her gently.

Finally she sat up, confused. "Who - What — What is going on?" She saw me and gave a little jump, and then she must have remembered who I was, because she calmed down a little and lay back on her pillow. "What is going on, Modesty?" she said sleepily. "I mean, Janie."

"Penelope! It's an emergency! Your parents came down to the barn and found Sheila! They know we're not Emily Hodgson's granddaughters, and they're taking her there right now!"

Penelope sat up again abruptly. "What?" she said. Her face had gone pale. "Then why are you here? Why did they not take you with them?"

I flushed. "I was outside, um, you know -"

She nodded.

"Well, we don't have any time to lose! You must give me my things right away, and we must go after them!"

Penelope nodded again. "Yes, if my parents find out that I fibbed to them,

I will be punished very severely! Let us go right away!"

I looked at her and shook my head. Was her stupid punishment all she cared about? What about us?

She climbed out of bed and yawned, reaching for her bathrobe. She was moving *way* too slowly. *You're killing me, Penelope*, I thought. *Can't you go any faster?* She was one stubborn girl, that was for sure.

"Um, do you think you could hurry it up a bit?" I finally said.

"I am going as fast as I can!" She yawned again. But she threw on her dress and pulled a pile of things out from under her bed, pushing them in my direction. "Here are your clothes."

I glanced around for a place to change and realized I'd have to do it right where I was. I pulled on my jeans under my dress and thrust my hand into the pocket, breathing only once my hand felt the cool, smooth medallion. I was flooded with relief. We could do this.

I quickly put on my shirt and handed the dress back to Penelope. Then, as I rolled Sheila's clothes up into a bundle, something heavy dropped to the floor. *Her cellphone!* I reached down and scooped it up quickly, stuffing it into my pocket and hoping desperately that Penelope hadn't noticed. Granted, it would be pretty interesting to see what Miss Penelope had to say about *that*, but we really didn't have any time for games.

We raced down the stairs and Penelope shouted back at me, "We will ride George together. Maybe if we get there before my parents, we can convince the crazy, old lady to tell them she is your grandmother. You know, she probably *is* a witch."

I gulped. I'd been to horseback riding camp a few times, but we only ever walked or trotted - we never galloped, and we ALWAYS wore proper riding gear. I had a feeling being careful wasn't Penelope's strong point.

I climbed gingerly onto the horse behind Penelope, and she turned and grinned at me mischievously. "I hope you are ready." And then, without even waiting for my reply she shouted, "Giddy up!" and pulled the horse's reins. I braced myself, closing my eyes tightly and clutching on to her waist so hard my fingers started to hurt. But then, as we gained speed, I began to relax. This was actually kind of fun. I had no choice to but to trust Penelope, and it was a good feeling to finally let go for a few minutes.

I smiled as the cool wind blew my hair back out of my face, and turned my head slightly to watch the scenery race by. There were lots of farmhouses and *tons* of animals, and in the distance I could even see the edges of the forest we had first arrived in.

We rode in silence, and about fifteen minutes later we started slowing down in front of a large, dark house with broken shutters and a red fence that looked sorely in need of repair. I drew in a sharp breath. Penelope's parents' carriage was parked in front of the house. We hadn't beaten them, after all.

We climbed off the horse, and Penelope motioned for me to follow her, placing a finger over her lips. "We must find a place to tie him up," she whispered. As we made our way quietly around to the back of the house, I tried desperately to come up with a plan. Should I just walk in, grab Sheila and use the medallion in front of everyone? Or should I try and play it cool?

Penelope found a place for George and then crouched under a large open window. "I can hear them," she whispered.

I crouched down next to her and could just barely make out the voice of a man coming from inside the house. "So of course, we thought it best to come right over here and find out if their story was true," he was saying.

There was a long silence. And then, unbelievably, there came the calm voice of an older woman. "Yes, yes, of course. I can understand your concern," she murmured. "But have no fear. My granddaughter is sleeping upstairs. We mustn't bother her."

My eyes practically bugged out of my head and I stared at Penelope. She was staring back at me, her mouth open.

"Yes, indeed, this darling girl is my granddaughter," the voice continued. "I thank you so very much for bringing her home this morning, she gets into the most terrible mischief!"

Penelope was still staring at me. "I - I don't understand," she stammered.

I shrugged. "I don't either."

"Is she really your grandmother?" Her eyes widened, and she took a step back from me. "A-a-re you a witch?"

I chuckled softly. "No," I said firmly. "I am most certainly not a witch!" I stood up and brushed myself off, waiting until I heard the door open and close and the sound of horses trotting away from the house. Then I motioned to Penelope. "Come with me," I said.

I strode up to the front door, squared my shoulders and knocked loudly. Penelope was standing behind me, looking for once like she had no idea what to do with herself. Her hands kept fluttering from her apron pockets to her bonnet and back again, and she coughed nervously.

A moment later the door swung open and an elderly woman peered out, looking suspiciously from side to side. She was tall and thin, and she was wearing the same dark dress, apron and bonnet that Penelope and her mother wore. Her eyes locked with mine, and she stared at me so intently, I felt like she could read my mind. Finally, after studying us for several seconds, she waved us inside, slamming the door behind us.

We followed her into the living room, which was a bare and empty space with just a few chairs in it. And in the corner, biting her nails and looking like she was going to pass out, sat a very pale and very small looking Sheila.

"You are not my granddaughters." The woman said it simply, sitting down and crossing her legs. Her eyes kept wandering back to my jeans.

"Yes, ma'am," I said, sliding into one of the remaining chairs. Penelope stayed standing near the doorway, clutching her bonnet in her white-knuckled hands. "I apologize. We, um…"

"Never mind!" The woman waved her hand in the air. "It doesn't matter. I must admit, I was very taken aback when Mr. and Mrs. Padgett brought you here. I may not know a lot about myself, but one thing I do know - I am no grandmother! But you seem like good kids, and if you are hiding from something, who am I to blow your cover?"

"Blow their cover?" Penelope broke in suddenly. "What does that mean?"

I stole a glance at Sheila. I'm no expert on languages, but I'm pretty sure people didn't use that expression in 1739. Sheila didn't seem to notice, though. She was still staring ahead and biting her nails.

The woman seemed flustered. "Er, I mean - I did not want to reveal your deception. However, it is best that you move on now. I shall bring you some tea and then you should be on your way." She stood up and walked out of the room, leaving Sheila, Penelope and me alone.

I stood up and rushed over to Sheila, leaning over to give her a big hug. "I have the medallion," I whispered in her ear. "Come on, it's time."

She stood up, and we both faced Penelope. "You're not going to understand this, but we need to leave now." I reached over and kissed her on her cheek. "You have been very kind to us, and we wish you all the best."

Penelope smiled at us. "I shall miss you," she said.

"We'll miss you too," Sheila replied. "And by the way, definitely keep on learning to read. Where we come from, girls can do everything boys can do, and you should stick up for yourself!"

With that, I took the medallion out of my pocket, grabbed Sheila's hand, and cried, "March 14, 2011! March 14, 2011! March 14, 2011!"

******

♥ March 15, 2011 ♥

Dear Diary,

So that's the whole crazy story. I can't believe I wrote it all down yesterday! My hand is killing me. It's practically falling off from writing so much.

We landed right back in the clubhouse, and it was like we had never left - It was still Monday afternoon, and even our leftover snack was still there! Thankfully, it seemed that nobody had even noticed we were gone.

The only problem was that Sheila was still wearing the apron and dress we had gotten from Penelope. And her regular clothes must have gotten lost in the race to Mrs. Hodgson's house. We couldn't find them anywhere!

I gave Sheila some normal clothes, but before she had time to change, SRJ burst into the room, took one look at her and started shrieking. "It's not fair!" he yelled. "I want a costume too!"

Luckily, I was able to distract him with an old Superman costume from the playroom. Sheila chuckled as she pulled on a pair of my jeans. "Things sure haven't changed around here," she said.

I rolled my eyes. "That's for sure." As I stuffed Penelope's old dress onto a shelf in the back of my closet, I felt something in the apron pocket, and pulled out the old newspaper Sheila had taken from Penelope's room. I unfolded it and shuddered as I looked at the date: July 5th, 1739.

The mind boggles.

******

At school today the minutes ticked by so slowly, I thought I would scream. But in history class, something happened that caught my attention.

We were sitting in third period, reading from our textbooks, and my eyes kept closing in spite of themselves. I was e-x-h-a-u-s-t-e-d! I had just started dozing off, when Mrs. Santini said, "Ok, class, turn the page. Who can read to us about Penelope Barker and the Edenton Tea Party?"

My ears perked up. Penelope? Edenton?

"Sheila, would you do the honors?"

Sheila straightened up in her chair and started randomly flipping through the pages of her book. She had that deer-in-headlights look kids get when they've been caught daydreaming. Finally, she gave Mrs. Santini a sheepish smile. "Um, what page were we on again?" A titter went through the room, and out of the corner of my eye, I could see MTS and Jessica giggling.

"Page 345, Sheila." Mrs. Santini shook her head.

Sheila cleared her throat and began reading: "Penelope Barker was born on June 17, 1728 in Edenton, North Carolina. Born Penelope Padgett, her parents were Samuel Padgett, a doctor and planter, and Elizabeth Blount, the daughter of an important politician. Remembered as a dutiful and well-behaved child, Penelope had two sisters, Elizabeth and Margaret."

I sat bolt upright in my chair and did a quick calculation in my head. 1728??? That would mean the Penelope Padgett in our textbook would have been... *eleven* in 1739. I swallowed hard, excitement rising in my chest, and turned to face Sheila, willing her to look up at me. But she just kept on reading, her voice betraying a light tremor.

"Unfortunately, Penelope Padgett suffered through many tragic events when she was just a teenager. Her father and her sister Elizabeth both d-d-died, and Penelope took responsibility for Elizabeth's children, Isabella, Robert and John. Several years later, she married her sister's widower, John Hodgson, and had two more sons of her own, Samuel and Thomas. Her husband died just a year after marrying her, leaving her to care for five children all on her own. She later remarried two more times."

Wow. It sounded like Penelope had had a really hard life! But wait a minute… I raised my hand. "Um, Mrs. Santini?"

"Yes, Janie," Mrs. Santini said, looking up from her textbook and frowning in my direction. "What is it?"

"Well, it's just – There's a mistake in the book." I drummed my fingers nervously on my desk. I'm not one of those kids that raises their hand all the time in class, and to be honest, talking in front of everybody makes me a bit nervous. I don't know why, but it does.

"A mistake?" Mrs. Santini was still frowning.

I glanced over at Sheila, and she grinned at me.

"Well, it's just that – Penelope's sisters' names were Elizabeth and Sarah. Not Margaret."

Mrs. Santini just kind of stood there for a few seconds. Then she said, "How could you possibly know a thing like that?"

"I, um, read a book about her once."

"Well, Janie, this is a very good textbook, and it doesn't usually make mistakes. You're probably misremembering." Mrs. Santini smiled kindly.

My face grew hot. "Um, actually, I'm pretty sure I'm not."

Mrs. Santini blinked several times, looking nonplussed. Finally, she said, "Well, Janie, since you seem so certain, why don't you Google it for us now at the class computer station?" She had her hand on her hip, and she was watching me expectantly.

Oh no. I got up slowly, trying to ignore the sinking feeling in my stomach, and made my way over to the computer station. Suddenly I wasn't so sure of myself. What if the history books got it wrong, or she had another sister? Mrs. Santini turned on the projector while I double clicked on the internet browser and carefully typed in the name "Penelope Barker". I don't think I ever remember the class so quiet – I swear, you could hear a pin drop!

I opened the Wikipedia entry and quickly scanned the page, dismayed to discover that it didn't mention any sisters. I closed it and went on to the next search result, a lump rising in my throat. And then, before I even started reading, Ben White pointed excitedly at the whiteboard.

"Mrs. Santini, I see it! Janie's right!"

Sure enough, there it was: Elizabeth and Sarah. I breathed a sigh of relief leaned back in my chair, a triumphant smile on my face.

Mrs. Santini regarded me with surprise. "Well, Janie, I had no idea we had an expert on Penelope Barker in our class! I guess we'll have to write to the textbook company and point out their error!"

I nodded, and as I headed back to my seat, I couldn't help adding under my breath, "Yeah, and she wasn't all that dutiful and well-behaved, either."

Mrs. Santini nodded to Sheila to keep on reading, and she cleared her throat and picked up the book:

"In October 1774, several months after the famous Boston Tea Party, in which American colonists destroyed tea cargo to protest the taxes they had to pay to the British king, Barker organized a women's protest of her own.

She wrote a statement calling for people to stop using British goods, and got 51 local women to sign it. A famous female activist in the period leading up to the American Revolution, Barker was reported to have said, 'Maybe it has only been men who have protested the king up to now. That only means we women have taken too long to let our voices be heard. We are signing our names to a document, not hiding ourselves behind costumes like the men in Boston did at their tea party. The British will know who we are. Patience and Modesty have been my inspiration.'"

Sheila stopped reading, her mouth open, and met my eyes. I grinned at her. Patience and Modesty, indeed. Now *that* sounded like the Penelope I knew. And clearly, she had learned how to read.

******

♥ **March 17, 2011** ♥

Dear Diary,

Yesterday Sheila couldn't come over after school, so we had to wait until this afternoon to meet up in the clubhouse and talk about everything that's been going on.

"We should go on another adventure!" Sheila said, plopping down on the floor.

"Hold your horses," I said. "We just barely made it back from the last one!"

Sheila giggled. "I mean a different kind of adventure. Something a bit less - dramatic." She held her hand out. "Can I see the medallion?"

I blinked. "Uh, I guess so," I said, reaching into my pocket and pulling it out. "But no funny business, ok?"

"No funny business," Sheila agreed, a tiny smile playing on her lips. She took the medallion and turned it around in her hands. And then, before I could stop her, she grabbed my arm. "June 21st, 1985! June 21st, 1985! June 21st, 1985!"

******

This time we landed in a green, grassy meadow in the middle of nowhere.

Sheila stood up and straightened her shirt, holding out her hand to help me up. I turned away from her, clenching my fists in anger. "I can't believe you did that," I muttered under my breath. "Sometimes you are such a total -"

"Oh, come on," she said, "Don't worry so much! This'll be fun!" She looked around and pointed to a bus stop about 300 yards away. In the distance, I could hear a truck speeding by. "Let's go see if there's a sign over there or anything," she said. "Oh, come on, Janie, I promise that the first second anything looks wrong, we'll leave right away. Don't be such a spoil sport!"

She held up the medallion, allowing the light to reflect off its shiny surface. It shone brightly in the sun. Then she handed it to me. "Here. I'm sorry, I shouldn't have done that."

"You can say that again," I said, shaking my head. I put the medallion in my pocket and stood up grumpily, feeling queasy. "I guess we could explore a little. But then we're going right home!" Sheila was acting like a little kid!

We trudged towards the bus stop in an uneasy silence, and I unzipped my sweatshirt, taking it off and tying it absentmindedly around my waist. At least here I wouldn't have to wear any old dresses with *bonnets*.

"Wow, look at that!" Sheila said, pointing excitedly at the bus stop. "They have an ad for that old movie we saw on Netflix with your parents last week!"

I stared at the placard. *Back to the Future – Coming Soon to a Theater Near You.*

"Didn't your mom say that that movie came out when she was eleven?" Sheila was saying. "I wonder what she was like at our age..." Her voice trailed off. Then her eyes grew wide. "Wait a minute! She grew up in your house, didn't she?"

"Oh no you don't!" I said firmly. "Don't even think about that. It would be *way* too creepy. Plus, we don't have any idea where we are." *I don't want to see what my house looked like when my mother was little, anyway,* I thought. *Her room was probably spotless.* "I think we should just go home now."

I stopped abruptly and grabbed Sheila's arm, motioning her to be quiet, as a group of five girls approached the bus stop. They looked young – maybe eight or nine years old – and they were talking excitedly. Luckily, they were too wrapped up in their conversation to notice us.

"I'm getting a Walkman for my birthday!" one of them was saying proudly. She had big, puffy blonde hair and a tiny button nose, and was wearing a jeans jacket and bright, pink leg warmers. *Leg warmers in the summer?* I found myself wondering. Sometimes I have the most random thoughts.

"That's awesome!" a second girl said. She was shorter, with brown hair and glasses, and she looked oddly familiar. "My big sister has one, and I'm totally jealous! She screams at me every time I go near it. I totally hope I get one for my birthday next year."

How many times could someone use the word "totally" in one sentence?

"What are you doing for your birthday party?" a third girl with big bangs asked.

"Oh, I'm just going to have a few kids over for a movie night. We're gonna watch a movie on the VCR! Don't worry, you guys are all invited."

The girls grew quiet as three older kids, holding enormous Slurpees in old-fashioned cups, came and sat down on the bench next to them. "Move your stuff over!" one of them said rudely, pushing the girls' bags onto the ground. "Do you think you guys own this bus stop?"

"Hey!" the short, familiar girl said, picking up her bag from the floor. "What's wrong with you guys? You could have just asked."

"*What's wrong with you guys!*" the older kid mimicked. His friends laughed.

Seriously? These kids were at least two or three years older than the girls. They looked our age. Were they really trying to pick a fight with them? *Who does that?* Sheila and I exchanged worried glances, and I had a sudden memory of the time RJ was pushed off a swing by a bigger kid and needed three stitches in his eyebrow.

"Hey, pick on someone your own size!" I was startled to hear the sound of my own voice. *Had I just said that?* The older kids stared at me, not saying anything, and Sheila looked as if she was going to faint. The short girl just stood there, gaping at me with her mouth open.

The minutes dragged on in silence, until a bus finally pulled into the stop and the older kids got on. The girls were noticeably relieved.

"Hey, you look a lot like my sister," the short girl said, smiling at me as she followed her friends onto a second bus that had pulled up behind the first. "I don't know if she would have stuck up for me like that, though."

Why did she look so familiar?

I was getting that queasy feeling again, and I suddenly realized that I had to get out of there, pronto. Without another word, I reached into my pocket and grabbed the medallion, placing my hand on Sheila's shoulder. "March 14, 2011!"

******

Again we screamed, as we felt ourselves falling.

Thump. We landed hard and looked around, surprised and relieved to find ourselves sprawled out on the floor of the clubhouse.

"Holy Smokes!" Sheila said, picking herself up off the ground and staring at the medallion with wonder.

I stayed where I was on the floor, too shocked to say anything. No matter how many times we did that, I didn't think I'd ever get used to it.

"Do you realize what this means, Janie?" Sheila said, looking from the medallion to me and back again. She jumped up and down and squealed with excitement. "This is going to be *so much fun!* We can travel through time, go wherever we want, and when we want to come home, all we have to do is say so!" She did a little dance.

I coughed and blinked, trying to focus and wondering vaguely why the room looked as if it had just had a new coat of paint.

"Sheila?" I could hear what sounded like my mother's voice calling from inside the house. "Sheila, I need your help, sweetie! Come on out of the clubhouse now, ok?"

"We're coming," I answered, looking at Sheila with a puzzled expression. I opened the door and walked outside. Why was my mother calling Sheila?

"Sheila!" It was my mother's voice again, but when I saw her, I realized that something was terribly wrong. She may have been calling Sheila, but she was looking straight at me.

TO BE CONTINUED…

******

The Day My Mom

Got Grounded!

♥ March 20, 2011 ♥

Dear Diary,

I don't really have that much time to write today, and I still haven't finished telling you the story! So before SRJ comes in to bother me, I'll try to get down as much as I can…

*****

So there we were, standing outside the clubhouse, and my mom was asking me to clean my room - but for some reason, she kept calling me Sheila!

Before I could reply, she turned around and hurried back towards the house. "Your father is having an important client over for dinner tonight," she called out over her shoulder, as she opened the screen door. "I need you to clean your room and help me straighten the living room, ok?"

I managed a nod and looked over at Sheila, who was standing right behind me with her mouth open. We stared at each other.

"Your mom looks kind of weird, doesn't she," Sheila finally said. "Did she color her hair?"

"Her hair?" I replied, annoyed. "Her *hair*? How can you think about her *hair* at a time like this?"

"Sorry," Sheila grinned sheepishly. "I just meant, she doesn't look like herself. And why did she call you Sheila?"

"I don't know, maybe she just mixed up our names." I picked up the medallion and dropped it into my pocket. "She always calls me Karen and she sometimes even calls my Dad RJ. Anyway, come on – let's go to my room so we can talk while I clean it up. We have a lot to talk about!"

"We sure do," Sheila agreed.

******

We walked inside and I gasped, looking around. Where was our piano? And why were the living room walls *peach*? Sheila tapped me on the shoulder, a worried look on her face. "This doesn't look right."

"No," I murmured. "It doesn't. And it doesn't *smell* right either." It smelled like strawberries, like – *Grandma Sollie*. For no reason, I had a sudden image of the cheese and tomato sandwiches with the crusts cut off that Grandma always made when I came over to her house after kindergarten, when I was little. And of the way my mom cried when she came back from the hospital when I was nine and told me that Grandma had died. A wistful knot formed in my stomach.

I walked over to the bookshelf in the far corner of the room – the old bookshelf, then chipped and sagging, that my parents had ultimately decided to throw out when we moved in. I remembered that bookshelf. Except now it was brand new…

"Sheila, what on Earth are you doing?" I was startled out of my thoughts by the sound of my mother's voice. "And what are you wearing? Go upstairs right now, change your clothes, and clean up that mess of yours. Honestly!"

She called me Sheila again.

I looked into my mother's eyes, and suddenly it all became shockingly, horrifyingly clear. *This wasn't my mother. It was Grandma Sollie!* Somehow, instead of going home, we had ended up in my grandparents' house, and we were still in the past!

****

I stared at Grandma Sollie, too stunned to say anything. She was younger, and she looked a lot like my mom – but now that I was really looking, I could see it was definitely her. Tears welled up in my eyes as I resisted an overwhelming urge to throw myself into her arms and hug her. I couldn't do that, at least not yet.

"Uh… O.K. uh…Mom," I cleared my throat, turning around and beckoning to Sheila. "I'm going upstairs now and I'll, uh, clean up my room right away."

I walked toward the stairs, grabbing Sheila by the arm and pulling her behind me. "We *have* to talk," I whispered loudly. "Come on!"

The stairs looked just like they did in my house, except that they were covered in soft, blue carpeting. Old-fashioned looking pictures hung on the wall. The one of my mom and Auntie Karen eating ice-cream cones outside on the front steps, which hung over the piano in our house. One I hadn't seen before of Grandpa Charlie when he was younger, holding up some kind of a trophy. One of Grandma Sollie, holding Grandpa Charlie's hand and looking incredibly happy.

And one of a girl about eleven years old, holding a dog on a leash and grinning. And I'll be a monkey's uncle if she didn't look incredibly, exactly, astoundingly *just like me*.

I paused in front of the picture of Auntie Karen, taking in her brown hair and glasses and shuddering as I remembered the girl at the bus stop.

"What in the world is going on here?" Sheila stage-whispered, as we reached the top of the stairs.

"Shhh!" I hissed. "Just wait a second." I yanked Sheila in the direction of what I hoped and guessed would be my mother's room. The door was closed and it had a big sign on it with a picture of a stop sign and the words DO NOT ENTER!! scrawled across it in bold, red crayon. I ignored the sign and pulled the door open, gasping yet again as I looked inside.

My mother's room was a mess.

******

"Somehow we've ended up in my grandparents' house!" I started to explain as I flopped down on my mother's bed, pushing a pile of (dirty?) laundry onto the floor.

As I spoke, I glanced around the room nervously. A bunch of posters hung on the wall – The Beatles, Madonna, and a few others I didn't recognize – and a huge box of old cassette tapes lay open on the floor. I had never listened to a tape before. My parents had a whole collection, which I looked through one day when I was bored, but my mom's old tape player didn't work. A collection of stuffed animals and funny looking dolls was strewn across the carpet, near the closet. A pink girl's desk stood in the corner, buried under piles of paper and books.

"Your grandparents?" Sheila looked blank for a moment as it sunk in. "Oh! So that's why she called you Sheila! She thought you were your... Wow." She leaned back on the bedpost, which was also pink, and swung her feet onto the bed.

"Don't put your shoes on the bed," I said automatically, tapping her feet.

"Seriously? Have you seen this place?" She gestured to the desk, and then to the closet which was literally overflowing with piles of clothes. "I really don't think shoes on the bed are an issue."

"I guess you're right. I can't believe it though…" *Who would have thought my mom would be such a slob?*

Suddenly Sheila reached over and grabbed a small spiral notebook that was sitting on my mom's night table. It was also pink and had the words "My Diary – Top Secret!" written across the front in magic marker. Sheila turned it over in her hands, inspecting it. Then she looked up at me, raised an eyebrow and grinned.

"No!" I said instinctively, reaching out to grab the diary. "We are *not* reading my mom's secret diary! Imagine if she did that to me! I'd never forgive her."

Sheila moved her hand away, holding the diary above her head. "But this is different," she insisted. "Would you mind if time travelers from the future read *your* diary?" She smiled mischievously and awaited my reply.

I couldn't resist a smile. "I guess when you put it that way…" When would I ever have another opportunity to find out about my mom's innermost thoughts, and what she was like when she was my age? "Come to think of it, she has said a few times she wished she had saved her diaries for me. Grandma Sollie threw them out when my mom went to college."

"See! She wants you to read it! And anyway, we have a mystery on our hands. If we're gonna get out of here, we need all the information we can get!" Without waiting for me to answer, she opened the diary and started reading aloud.

I moved uncomfortably on the bed, an uncertain feeling in my gut. Reading someone else's diary was never right, and yet –

☼ *June 20, 1985* ☼

Dear Diary,

Ok, this is the last straw! Last night I came home from ballet and found Karen in my room, playing with my Barbie Dream House. I told her she could play with it sometimes, but only when I was home! She ran out when she saw me coming, but I could tell she moved the Barbie furniture around and ruined my setup. I made a new DO NOT ENTER sign, and if that doesn't work, I'll have to think of something else.

Marcy was supposed to come over today and bake cookies with me, but at the last minute she told me she had decided to go over to Jen's house. ☹ I think we're still best friends, but lately she always seems to want to be with Jen. She says it's just easier to go over to Jen's because she lives closer. Sometimes it seems like me and Jen are fighting over Marcy, and it's soooooo unfair. Why can't I ever be the one they're fighting over?

******

Sheila stopped reading and looked up at me. "Wow. Your mom sounds like a real kid!"

"What do you mean, dork brain? She is a real kid! What do you think, that she was born a grownup?"

Sheila rolled her eyes and flipped a few pages back. She continued to read:

☼ *March 13, 1985* ☼

Dear Diary,

Dad's been acting really weird lately. Yesterday, I went into his study when he wasn't home to find my Sweet Valley High book. There was no one there, so I sat down to read on the couch. And then, suddenly when I looked up, he was standing there, totally out of breath. It was s-t-r-a-n-g-e! When he saw me, he went totally white and started muttering something about running up the stairs. Which was weird, because his study's on the first floor.

Then this morning, he told me that he needed to talk to me about something after school. He looked very serious, like when I got a C- on my math test last month. Except he wasn't angry. I have to —

*****

Sheila stopped midsentence and snapped the book shut, as the door swung open. I looked up, startled.

"Sheila! You haven't even started cleaning your room!" Grandma Sollie had the same expression on her face that my mom did, when she was really exasperated. "Well, there's no time for that now." She looked at her watch and back at me. "You have to be at ballet practice in fifteen minutes. Get your stuff together, we'll be leaving in five. And don't forget to brush your hair."

She turned sharply and left the room, closing the door behind her. I looked around, frantically searching for my mom's ballet stuff. My mom was forever trying to convince me to take ballet lessons, but I never wanted to. Too prissy.

I spotted a small, pink backpack slung across the desk chair. As I ruffled inside, I saw with relief that it contained a white leotard and a pink tutu. I made a face at Sheila. "She sure does like pink."

"Yeah," Sheila answered, wrinkling her nose. "I'm glad *I'm* not gonna have to wear that."

"That's going to be the least of my troubles," I said. "You may not remember this, but I don't actually *know* any ballet. How am I going to get through a whole class? And anyway – where *is* she?!"

"I don't know…" Sheila said, "And what if she's there?"

"I guess we're just going to have to go and find out."

******

"Ok, we're ready!" I called out to Grandma Sollie, as we came down the stairs. "Shei— I mean, Susan's parents are coming home late today, so she'd like to come with me to ballet. S-s-Susan's new at school."

Grandma Sollie smiled at Sheila and shrugged her shoulders. "Nice to meet you, honey. I don't see any problem with that. As long as it's ok with your parents."

"Oh, it is." Sheila grinned at me.

We climbed into the back seat of the old-fashioned, blue Honda parked in front of the house and put on our seatbelts.

"I'm glad to see you're buckling up, girls, but I'm not sure it's necessary in the back seat." We glanced at each other. *Weird.*

As we slowly made our way across town, I looked out the window with my mouth open. We passed the 7-11 on Montrose Road that had been there as long as I could remember — and it looked almost exactly the same, just newer somehow. The Barnes and Noble that had been next door was gone, replaced by something called Crowne Books. Or rather — Crowne books was to be replaced by Barnes and Noble, sometime in the future.

Then we passed a big, empty lot on the right, and Sheila nudged me. "Montgomery Mall is gone!" she whispered.

"You mean it hasn't been built yet," I whispered back. We giggled.

At last we pulled up in front what used to be — or rather, what would become -- The Bagel Place. Except it was painted orange and had a big green sign on it that read, "Molly's Ballet".

"Ok, girls," Grandma Sollie called as we got out of the car. "Your father will be here to pick you up at five-thirty sharp. Don't hold him up. He has an important dinner tonight."

******

Inside, everybody seemed to know where to go. We stood uncertainly by the door, trying not to look too confused, when a girl with straight black hair, braces and a huge smile bounded up to us.

"Oh my God, Sheila! You are *not* going to believe what Kevin said to me this morning. Where *were* you? I thought you were sick or something." Without waiting for a reply, she grabbed my hand and pulled me toward the locker room. "Come on, let's go get dressed."

When she saw Sheila following us, the girl turned to her and demanded, "Who are you?"

"This is my cousin Susan," I managed. "She's visiting from Detroit."

"Nice to meet you, Susan." The girl stuck out her hand and shook Sheila's hand matter-of-factly. Then she turned to me, an accusing look on her face. "You never told me you had a cousin your age that lived in Detroit! So, you want to watch the class?" She rolled her eyes. "It's pretty boring. Sheila and I have wanted to quit for ages, but our parents won't let us."

Now *this* was getting interesting. My mom was always telling me how much she loved ballet when she was my age. I grinned to myself. My mom was cool. I tried to remember if she had ever mentioned a friend who took ballet lessons with her, but my mind came up blank.

"I'll just listen to my ipod, or whatev – Ow!!" Sheila shot me a questioning look, as I elbowed her sharply in the ribs.

"Uh…" I croaked, then cleared my throat. "Shei – I mean – Susan has been thinking of taking ballet lessons."

The girl looked at me, then at Sheila, and then back at me again. "Ok, whatever. Come on, let's go get dressed."

******

"Sheila, what's wrong with you today?" Molly, the ballet teacher, stood next to me and frowned. "It's almost as if you don't remember any of the steps! Here, let me show you." She held my waist and pointed with her foot. "See, it's like this. One, two, three. One two three."

I cast a worried glance at Sheila. It was hopeless. I couldn't dance if my life depended on it.

"Marcy, what's wrong with Sheila today?" a girl with long, blond curls called out from the other side of the studio. The girls standing next to her snickered. "It's like she has *three* left feet, instead of her usual two."

"Shut up, Jen," Marcy looked at me, uncomfortable. "I don't know why Jen has to be so mean. I wish you guys could become friends."

So this was my mom's best friend Marcy. And Jen - the girl from the diary who was trying to steal Marcy away!

"Well, she's right." I brushed the hair away from my eyes and put on my best brave grin. "I haven't been practicing lately, and I'm not myself today."

"I'll say," Marcy said, doing a pirouette, her straight, black hair whirling behind her. "If I didn't know any better, I'd say you'd been kidnapped by aliens and replaced by a clone."

Sheila coughed and looked at me, raising her eyebrow. "Yeah, Marcy. Sheila really hasn't been herself lately."

******

Back in the locker room, Marcy was very quiet as she changed back into her jeans and tee-shirt. I could feel her staring at me, but every time I turned around, she immediately looked away. Finally, she spoke.

"Did you tell your parents about the A you got on our math test last week?"

"Uh, yeah." I answered, pulling on my socks. "My dad was really happy. I don't think I've ever – "

"We didn't *have* a math test last week." Marcy faced me squarely, arms folded across her chest. "And you've never gotten an A in math in your life! What the heck is going on here, Sheila? Or whoever you are!"

I sank onto the bench, putting my sneaker down and trying desperately to decide what to tell her. If I told her the truth, would she even believe me?

And what if she blabbed about it to other people? On the other hand, maybe if she knew what was going on, she could help us get home.

"Ok." I picked up my sneaker and started putting it on again. "I'll tell you, but you have to promise not to tell anyone. And I'm warning you – you're probably not going to believe me."

******

The three of us walked outside, nobody saying anything. Marcy kept looking from me to Sheila, shaking her head wordlessly. Then she cleared her throat. "So, um, maybe you guys should come over to my house, so we can talk."

Sheila nodded her head. "That sounds like a good idea," she said before I had a chance to answer. Just then, the old blue Honda pulled up at the curb. The man inside leaned over and rolled down the window.

Grandpa Charlie!

My mouth dropped open as I stared at him. He looked almost exactly as I remembered him from all the pictures we had at home, except much younger. He was wearing a button-down, striped shirt with a tie, and brown pants and sneakers. And a huge smile creased his face.

"Sheila!" he exclaimed. He was positively beaming. "You have no idea how happy I am to see you! I was worried sick!" His face grew sterner, and he gestured to Sheila. "When your friend goes home, we're going to have to have a little talk. You have what you took from me, right?"

Sheila and I exchanged worried glances. *What I took?*

"Uh.." I barely managed a croak. "Sure. I think so. But Dad," I swallowed hard. "Marcy invited us over for dinner. Would that be ok? We can talk later, when I get home."

Grandpa Charlie sighed. "Sheila, I really wish you'd tell me these things before I drag out to pick you up – especially on a day like today. I guess it's ok, though. Call me when you're ready to come home."

******

"So basically, yeah, we're time-travelers from the future, and I'm Sheila's daughter." I stuck out my hand. "My name's Janie. Nice to meet you. And her real name is Sheila."

We were sitting in Marcy's room, on the thick, purple carpet that covered her floor. Thank goodness it wasn't pink. I had explained the entire situation to her, even pulling out the medallion to show her the inscription. She had listened carefully, interrupting only to ask the occasional question.

She reached out and shook my hand, her eyes wide. "Jeez. I … I don't really know what to say. I'm not even sure I believe you."

"Well…" I pointed to Sheila's orange Crocs. "Have you ever seen shoes like this before?"

Marcy laughed. "I'd been wondering about those. No offence, but they're kind of ugly."

Sheila smiled. "Yeah. For some reason they're wildly popular in the future, though."

"But that isn't actual proof." Marcy continued. "How do I know you didn't just make those yourselves, or buy them in some kind of funky store?"

"Yeah…" I stared thoughtfully at the River Phoenix poster that hung on the wall next to her dresser. My mom had shown me the movie *Stand by Me* on Netflix, so I knew who River Phoenix was. She had told me he was one of her favorite actors when she was a kid. Then suddenly it hit me.

"Wait a minute – what's the date today?"

"June 22nd, why?" Marcy answered.

"Oh. My. God." I jumped up and started pacing around the room nervously. "Because I just realized, tomorrow – June 23rd – there is going to be a horrible plane crash! My mom's second cousin Emma, who lived in Ireland, was on that plane! My mom didn't know her very well, but we attend a memorial service for her every year, on June 23rd."

Sheila looked startled. "Your mom's cousin is supposed to be in a plane crash tomorrow?"

I sat back down, shaking, as the implications of what I was saying sank in. "We have to do something! Warn her not to get on the plane – or better yet, figure out how to delay or prevent the plane from taking off!"

Marcy was staring at me, her face frozen in a look of surprised panic.

"Please, Marcy," I pleaded with her. "You've got to believe us. I look just like my mom, right? And we're dressed funny, and when we have time, we'll tell you all about the internet, ipods, cell phones, and what happens in *Back to the Future*, which is coming out in a couple of weeks. I know it's a lot to ask, but I promise you, we'll be able to prove it to you eventually."

As I spoke, Sheila reached into her back pocket and pulled out her ipod. "I'm such a dummy, I can't believe I forgot about this." She turned it on and handed it to Marcy. "Here, listen to this."

Marcy's eyes widened even more, if that was even possible, as she put on

the earphones and listened. "It's like a tiny Discman!" she finally sputtered.

"And the sound is incredible!" She stood up and beckoned to us impatiently, suddenly all business. "All right guys, what we need now is a plan. First to save your cousin. And then to find your mom and get you guys back home."

******

♥ March 20, 2011 ♥

Dear Diary,

Yes, it's still today, Sunday. I haven't written this much in a million years! Then again, I guess this is the first time that something really interesting has happened to me. Not that my life isn't interesting, but you know what I mean. I had to take a break earlier, because SRJ came running into my room crying like a hysterical baby. When I asked him what was wrong, he just climbed up on my bed and sat there, sucking his thumb and clinging to his old baby blanket. After a few minutes, my mom came up after him, opening the door and sighing. It turned out all that crying was just because he couldn't have another chocolate-chip cookie. As if three cookies weren't enough! I'm telling you, that kid is spoiled. I *never* got more than two cookies when I was his age, and I didn't go around crying about it! My mom scooped him off the bed and carried him back downstairs, winking at me and apologizing for bursting into my room without knocking.

Things with my mom have been kind of different since I got back. But I'll tell you about that later.

Anyway, right after that I got a phone call, and you'll never guess who it was. CALVIN! He was calling me to get the English homework. He never knows what the homework is, and his backpack is always a mess. It's lucky he called me and not Sheila, though. If he had called her, she probably would have had a heart attack or something. And I'd never hear the end of it.

Speaking of Sheila, my hand is about to fall off, but I *have* to get to the end of the story. So we were in Marcy's room, remember? Trying to figure out how to save my cousin and find my mom …

******

"Marcy, Sheila's dad is here to pick her up!"

Marcy looked at me, panicked. "What should we do?" she whispered. "We still have to make a plan. And you definitely shouldn't go back to your grandparents' house. It took me *half an hour* to figure out you aren't Sheila. You'll be lucky if it takes them ten minutes!"

Sheila and I glanced at each other nervously.

"Marcy!" Marcy's mom called up the stairs again, her voice impatient. "Did you hear me? I said Sheila's dad is here to pick her up!"

Just then the door opened, and Grandpa Charlie walked in. He was wearing jeans and a red, plaid flannel shirt, and he had a faint, familiar smell. *Old Spice.* I closed my eyes and breathed in, suddenly struck by a vague memory of sitting in his lap on the swing in our backyard when I was really little, listening to him read *Blueberries for Sal.*

The sound of his voice jolted me back to reality. "Hi Marcy," he said, frowning at Sheila as she grabbed her ipod and stuffed it quickly into her back pocket. He turned to me. "Sheila, come on. We really have to get going. We have a lot to talk about!"

I just sat there, looking at Marcy, and then at Grandpa Charlie.

"Um," Marcy stood up and pulled at the leg of her jeans, scratching her ankle. "Actually, I was wondering if Ja – I mean, Sheila and Susan could sleep over tonight. We still have a lot of math homework to finish."

"I'm sorry, honey, she can't," Grandpa Charlie said, placing a firm hand on my shoulder. "We have to go home now." He leaned over and added quietly, "We need to talk about the medallion."

I gasped and jumped up as if stung by a bee. *He knew about the medallion.*

"H-h-h-h" I stuttered, then tried again. "How do you know about the medallion?"

The room was so quiet you could hear a pin drop. Grandpa Charlie looked at me quizzically, furrowing his brow and biting his thumbnail. When he spoke again, his voice was low.

"You're not Sheila." It was a statement rather than a question. His eyes darted from me to Sheila and then to Marcy. "Who are you?" he finally asked. "And where's Sheila?"

"Um." A sense of panic welled up inside me. "I-i-i don't know. I mean, I know who I am, of course. I, um, just don't know where Sheila is," I finished lamely.

"Janie found the medallion when she was seven, on a family vacation to Miami," Sheila broke in. I smiled at her gratefully as she continued. "It had her name on it and everything! I mean, it's not like we took it from anyone. The inscription on it was written in a secret language we made up together for our clubhouse, *four years* after she found it! It said, 'Janie, hold the medallion and say the date you want to visit three times' or something like that. Well, we did what it said, and we ended up in an open field, but then when we tried to go home, it brought us here! And before that we took a trip back to 1739!"

Again there was silence, and even though I was looking at Sheila, I could feel Grandpa Charlie's eyes boring into me.

"Janie." He said my name simply. I looked over at him and was shocked to see tears in his eyes. "I knew this could happen one day, but I never thought -" His voice caught, and I realized he was trying not to cry. "You're Sheila's girl. Of course! How could I have missed that? Come here sweetie."

He opened his arms, and as I leaned in and put my head on his shoulder, I knew everything was going to be ok.

******

"All right, girls," Grandpa Charlie sat down on Marcy's bed, moving aside a pile of *Seventeen* magazines. "I guess I'll just have to start at the beginning."

"Wait -" Marcy said. "My mom's expecting us to come down to dinner now. Does Sheila's mom know about the medallion too? And what about Karen?"

"No, Marcy, they don't." Grandpa Charlie stood back up. "Come to think of it, it might be a good idea for Sheila and Susan -" he paused, grinning sheepishly, "I mean, Janie and Sheila - to stay here tonight after all. We don't need to stir up any more trouble than we already have."

"I'm sure it'll be fine with my mom," Marcy said. "Why don't you guys go for a walk and talk things over. You can come back here after dinner, and we can make a plan." Marcy seemed to be a very sensible person. I could see why my mom liked her. She didn't freak out when things got weird, and she always seemed to know what to do. Come to think of it, she kind of reminded me of Sheila.

"Great plan." Grandpa Charlie reached over and tweaked Marcy's ear. Then he glanced at his watch, a ginormous one that seemed to double as a miniature calculator. "We'll be back in an hour."

******

I shivered as we walked down Marcy's street, making our way around old-fashioned parked cars, bicycles and the occasional motorcycle. It was cool for the end of June. Grandpa Charlie handed me his sweater, and I shrugged it on, pulling it tightly around me.

"The medallion has been in our family for generations," Grandpa Charlie began. "According to family legend, it originated in ancient Egypt, at the time of Ramses the Great. And it's been passed down ever since, from grandparent to grandchild, always skipping a generation."

"Why?" Sheila asked. "I mean, why doesn't it go from parent to child?"

"That's a good question, Sheila. Nobody really knows. The origins of the medallion remain shrouded in mystery. My guess is that it's meant to allow the family to maintain a semblance of normalcy. Each Bearer of the Medallion is born into a perfectly ordinary family, and it's only when they come of age that the medallion is passed on to them by their grandmother or grandfather."

"I wonder…" Sheila started saying.

"What?" my grandfather asked. "Please don't hesitate to ask."

"Well, when we were in 1739, we met this woman called Mrs. Hodgson. She was the one that helped us get away, and she said something strange that made us think she might not be from that time. Could she have been a Bearer of the Medallion?"

Grandpa Charlie frowned. "I don't know the answer to that off the top of my head. But it's certainly possible."

Bearer of the Medallion. It sounded so serious. "Ok," I said finally. "But it wasn't passed down to me by you. I just found it when we were on vacation in Miami. You aren't even-" I stopped midsentence, realizing the horrifying implications of what I was about to say.

Grandpa Charlie froze and looked up. "No. No. No matter how tempting, you must not tell me *anything* about the future. The space-time continuum is a very delicate matter. It must not be tampered with except under the most extraordinary circumstances." He continued walking. "Yes, the matter of passing on the medallion is a tricky one indeed. That's part of what I was trying to find out when Sheila – "

"What? What happened to my mother? Where is she?"

"I don't know," Grandpa Charlie answered gravely. "I was in my study, about to embark on a journey to ancient Egypt – when suddenly she burst in and grabbed the medallion at the very last second. Then, before I knew what was happening, she was gone." He looked directly at me and knelt down, holding my shoulders and looking into my eyes. "Janie, I don't know where your mother is. When I saw you, I assumed you were her, and that somehow she had managed to come back. But the medallion can only be used by or with the Bearers themselves. If Sheila's stuck back in ancient Egypt, she won't be able to use the medallion to come home!"

I stopped walking as the implications of what Grandpa Charlie was saying sank in. *She can't come home by herself, but we can go back and get her.*

Grandpa Charlie continued. "You mentioned that you tried to get home but ended up here instead. The medallion works in mysterious ways. I don't understand them all. Maybe it brought you here to save your mother!"

I shuddered, imagining my mom – or rather, a girl named Sheila who was a lot like me – stuck somewhere in ancient Egypt, alone and scared out of her mind. I glanced over at Sheila and she stared back at me, looking frightened for the first time since this whole thing had started. We had no time to lose.

******

As we headed back to Marcy's house, I remembered something.

"Uh, Grandpa, there's something else we need to do. There's going to be a horrible plane crash tomorrow -"

"Stop!" he cut me off, a wild look in his eyes. "You mustn't tell me *anything* about the future! Later, after we get your mom back, I'll explain more about the medallion and the rules we must abide by. But for now, let me make one thing clear: Interfering in the future is a very dangerous business! The tiniest little change can alter reality irreparably. Terrible things have happened when Bearers have had the hubris to believe they can engineer history!"

"What's hubris?" Sheila interrupted. That's one good thing about Sheila — she's never embarrassed to admit she doesn't know something. Her mom is always saying there's no such thing as a stupid question.

"Hubris means false pride," Grandpa explained. "Arrogance. Like when someone thinks they can do impossible things, and ends up just getting into trouble. It's important to believe in yourself, but hubris can be dangerous."

"But cousin Emma-" I stammered. "She's going to -"

"Enough! Whatever happened in your past is going to happen in our future. That's just the way the world works." But he was looking at me strangely. "Emma," he murmured softly. He was silent for several seconds before saying, "She's supposed to be flying home from New York tonight."

I felt a chill go up my spine.

"You said the space-time continuum shouldn't be tampered with *except in extraordinary circumstances*," Sheila broke in. "Aren't these extraordinary circumstances? Maybe we can't prevent the plane crash altogether, but we can try and make it so that Emma doesn't get on the plane!" She looked at Grandpa expectantly. "Maybe the medallion didn't bring us here just to save Janie's mom," she added. "Maybe it brought us here so we could save Emma too!" That's another good thing about Sheila – she's a very good arguer. Her dad always says she'll probably become a lawyer when she grows up.

"I don't know…" Grandpa's voice trailed off. "Maybe." He looked at his watch again, and I wondered vaguely why everyone in 1985 seemed to wear watches. Maybe it was because they didn't have cell phones and stuff. "Emma told me her flight is supposed to take off tonight, shortly after midnight," he continued. "You shouldn't have told me, but now that I know… I'll see what I can do. Meanwhile, you girls have to go back and get your mom. Get the medallion to take you to May 31, 1279 BC, the day Ramses the Great ascended the throne."

"But how do we make sure to end up where my mom is?" I asked. "I mean, we tell the medallion the date we want to visit, but not the place."

"You just need to worry about *when* you want to go," Grandpa answered. "The medallion will take care of the *where*."

******

We arrived back at Marcy's house just as they were finishing supper. "My mom said it was ok for you to stay over," Marcy said as she opened the door. "Come on, let's go up to my room."

As we walked up the stairs, I thought about everything that had happened that day. If someone had told me I'd be traveling through time with Sheila and hanging out with my mom's eleven year old best friend, I'd have said they were stark raving mad. I'm not a very brave person. I mean, I'm not a scaredy cat or anything, but I don't even go on roller coasters at the amusement park! They make me want to throw up. The last time we went to King's Dominion, Sheila went on all the rides, even the Anaconda and the Berserker. I was too chicken.

Marcy sat on her bed, eyes wide, as Sheila filled her in on what Grandpa Charlie had told us. As she was talking, I pulled the medallion out of my pocket and turned it over in my hands.

Posei: Kudm jenkjdy osm loy jki moji a fosj ju xelej jkzii jetil. Or in plain old English: **Janie: hold tightly and say the date u want to visit three times.**

I shuddered. *Bearer of the Medallion indeed.*

"So do we all go back together?" Marcy finally said, when Sheila had finished. "I mean, she may be your mom and all, but she *is* my best friend."

I shrugged my shoulders. "I don't know. I don't see why not."

"Yeah!" Sheila said, jumping up. "Let's all go! I think we're better off sticking together. And you're really good at solving problems," she added, looking at Marcy.

I felt a fluttering in my stomach as I stretched out my hands and held the medallion up in front of me. Sheila and Marcy reached out and grasped it as well. I closed my eyes as tightly as I could. "May 31, 1279 BC! May 31, 1279 BC! May 31, 1279 BC!"

*****

♥ March 21, 2011 ♥

Dear Diary,

OMG. I *seriously* hate Mondays.

First of all, it's the day we have to go back to school after the weekend. Not that I mind school that much, but still – weekends are much more fun. Second, we usually have more homework due on Mondays. I guess Mrs. Santini figures we have plenty of time to do homework over the weekend, which if you think about it, doesn't really make sense. And third, on Mondays I have piano lessons. I don't think I've told you that yet. My mom said that if I didn't take ballet, I had to take *something*, and I chose piano. I guess I don't actually hate it, but it's kind of a pain.

Yesterday I wrote so much that my hand almost fell off. But I still didn't get to the end of the story! I'm going to finish it today no matter what. So here goes…

******

We screamed as we felt ourselves falling, plunged back into the dark tunnel. I was vaguely aware of squeezing Marcy and Sheila's hands as hard as I could and yelling at the top of my lungs. And just when I thought I couldn't take even one more second -

Thud. We landed abruptly on what felt like a cold, marble floor. I opened my eyes, blinking to try and see where we were, but it was pitch black. I rubbed them and tried again. Nothing.

"Oh my gosh!" I heard Marcy exclaim. "What the -" She stopped midsentence. "I can't see anything! Can you guys see anything?"

"No," I answered, a knot of fear in my stomach. "This didn't happen last time. Last time we landed on a field in the middle of nowhere — and then in my mom's old clubhouse."

"Wait!" Sheila said suddenly, I think I see some light over there!"

I looked around me, trying to see what she was talking about. And sure enough, a tiny crack of light seemed to appear several feet away.

"I see it!" I cried excitedly. "Look, Marcy!"

We made our way carefully towards the light, and as we reached it I realized it was a tiny opening between two large, stone doors. Sheila reached out and gave one of them a gentle push. Sure enough, it swung open, and we were suddenly flooded with light.

And sound. And music. And —

I looked around, rubbed my eyes again and did a double take. The doors had opened up onto a beautiful, well-lit room, filled with tables of sumptuous food and dozens of people. In the far corner, on what seemed like a raised platform, sat a man in ancient Egyptian dress, holding what looked like a scepter. This is going to sound crazy, but it looked just like a scene from *Prince of Egypt*. As we stood there, frozen in shock, the room suddenly became completely silent. All eyes were on us.

A man standing in front of the doors began to talk excitedly, gesturing in our direction and bowing towards the figure on the raised platform. He was wearing a wrap-around skirt that was belted at the waist, and a striped, cloth headdress. He held a stick, which he was waving around in the air.

And this is the really freaky part. Even though he was speaking a foreign language, *I could understand almost everything he said!*

I looked at Sheila and Marcy, who were both frozen in place, watching him with their mouths open. If I hadn't been so scared, I probably would have burst into laughter.

"How dare you stand straight before the Pharaoh!" he was shouting, "All who come before him must bow!" He raised his stick threateningly and began walking towards us. The room filled with nervous chatter, and I took a step backwards.

"Wait!" The man on the raised platform stood, and the noise died down just as quickly as it had begun. "Look how they're dressed! They don't look like ordinary people. And see what she's holding!" He pointed his scepter in my direction. "It's a large coin, just like the one the Goddess brought us yesterday!" He reached into his tunic and pulled out a medallion. As he held it up in the air, the crowd began to chatter again.

A medallion! He had a medallion that looked just like mine!

As I stared at him, he reached out his hand as if to accept a gift. "We allow you to approach us and present us with your offering," he intoned.

Before I could say anything, Sheila grabbed my arm and pulled me back in the direction of the stone doors. "Come on guys," she whispered urgently. "We gotta get out of here. If he takes the medallion, we're finished."

******

We ran as fast as we could, not even stopping when we heard the doors slam behind us. It was pitch black again, and we had no idea where we were going. I'm not a very good runner. In gym class, I'm always one of the last people to be picked for a team (right before Ben White), and when we did the mile run, I walked most of the way. But now I ran as if my life depended on it.

"Wait!" Marcy called out, stopping and leaning forward with her hands on her knees. "I have asthma," she managed between breaths, "and I didn't bring my inhaler!"

I cast a worried glance at Sheila, but she grinned at me and started feeling around in her pockets. Eventually she pulled out a small, white inhaler. "I have asthma too," she said, handing the inhaler to Marcy. "You guys probably don't have Symbicort yet, but it works pretty well. Here, you just turn this little red thing on the bottom, and take it like a regular Ventolin puff."

Marcy accepted the inhaler and took a puff, handing it gratefully back to Sheila. "More proof you're from the future," she smiled, breathing more normally now. "As if I still needed it."

We all laughed, and it suddenly struck me that we weren't in total darkness anymore. I looked around, trying to figure out where the light was coming from, and noticed a small hole, just big enough to put my hand through, in the rock about three feet away. I walked towards it, peeking through in hopes of seeing what was on the other side. And what I saw nearly gave me a heart attack.

******

"Sh-sh-sh-sheila," I whispered loudly, beckoning for them to come over to me. "M-m-marcy, look!" I was so dumbstruck, I could barely speak.

On the other side of the wall sat a young girl, about our age, with a head of frizzy, brown hair tied up in a scrunchie. She seemed tired and haggard and looked as if she had been crying. Her jeans were torn, and she was wearing a pink tee-shirt that had WHAM written across the front in large, purple letters.

I stood back to let them look through the hole.

"Oh. My. Goodness." Marcy went white as a ghost. "It's Sheila! We've found her!"

My mom, eleven years old, was sitting on the other side of a stone wall, in a tunnel in ancient Egypt.

I must have fainted, because the next thing I knew, I was lying on the floor with my feet up, and Sheila was gently slapping my face.

"Janie, wake up!" she whispered urgently. "We've found your mother, and now we need to go home!"

I stood up shakily and peered through the hole again. The girl, hearing the commotion, had stood up and walked towards the wall.

"Hello?" she said, her voice incredulous. "Is somebody out there speaking English?"

"Sheila, it's me, Marcy! Reach out to me and hold my hand. We're gonna get you out of here!"

A sob came from the other side of the wall, and I realized my mom was crying again. "Oh, Marcy, thank goodness! They locked me up in here, and I thought I'd never get home. Oh, thank you!" I saw her hand reach out from the hole, and Marcy grasped onto it, holding it tightly.

Just then, I heard the faint sound of a man's voice echoing throughout the tunnel, speaking that strange foreign language. "They must have gone this way. There isn't any other way out of here!"

"Hurry!" I shouted, suddenly knowing exactly what needed to be done. "Grab onto the medallion!" I held it at the entrance to the hole, and waited until we were all holding onto it: Marcy, Sheila, my mother, and me. "June

22nd, 1985! June 22nd, 1985! June 22nd, 1985!"

******

This time I noticed the clubhouse didn't look anything like *my* clubhouse. First, the walls were – yup, you guessed it – pink. Ugh. Second, the posters were completely different. My J-Lo was gone, replaced with another Madonna, and an entire wall was covered with little pictures of really cute stuffed animals that said on them "Gotta Getta Gund" and looked as if they had been cut out of a magazine.

My mom stood up and brushed herself off, staring at me the entire time.

"Who are you?" she asked suspiciously. "Marcy, who are these people?"

Marcy looked at me and then at Sheila, stifling a laugh. "Well, you're not going to believe this, Sheila, but this is your daughter Janie, and her best friend Sheila."

I thought my mom's eyes were going to pop out of her head. They swept over me, inspecting my hair, my clothes and my shoes. Finally, she spoke. "This is incredibly weird. You look so much like me! If I hadn't just, uh, gotten back from ancient Egypt, I'd definitely think you were insane."

"Yeah," I smiled at her. "Me too." I was impressed by her calm, though. I'd had a whole lot more time to get used to the idea, and I was still freaking out.

"Your clothes are interesting. Not too different, but not the same, you know?"

Marcy put her hand on my mom's shoulder and grinned. "That's nothing. Wait until Sheila shows you her ipod."

"Her i-what?" My mom looked confused.

"Never mind," I said, laughing. You'll have enough time to get used to those in the future."

I bent over to tie my shoe, when the door to the clubhouse swung open, and Grandpa Charlie burst in.

"Oh, Sheila!" He ran over and gave her a huge hug, laughing and crying all at the same time. "Sheila! I was worried sick!" He stood back and looked at her, his face taking on a stern expression. "I still can't believe you did that. You're grounded, young lady! For ten days at least. And there will be absolutely no phone privileges for at least a week."

I grinned from ear to ear and pinched myself to keep from laughing. Seeing my mom get grounded – now *that* was interesting.

******

Grandpa Charlie sat across from me in my mother's room, as the story came tumbling out. "What are you going to do about your medallion?" I asked when I was done. "That Pharaoh guy in Egypt has it, and I don't think he's going to give it back anytime soon."

"That Pharaoh guy?" Grandpa repeated, raising an eyebrow in amusement. "You mean Ramses?"

"Uh, yeah." I flushed. I was nothing if not articulate.

"Honestly, I don't know. The important thing is that the medallion was successfully passed on to you. I don't think I need it anymore. And I think your mother has had enough adventure for the time being."

I giggled. I don't think I'll ever get used to thinking of my mom as a kid.

"Janie, you are now the only remaining Bearer of the Medallion. Being a Bearer carries a lot of responsibility." He reached over and handed me a folded piece of paper. "Read this when you get home," he said. He gave me a hug and kissed me on the cheek. "I love you, Janie. You're a wonderful kid. I'm proud of you, and I'm extremely proud of your mother for having raised a beautiful human being like yourself."

I flushed again and hugged him back, stuffing the note into my pocket. "I love you too, Grandpa."

******

Sheila and I made it back home in time for dinner that night. We were exhausted, but as far as anyone else knew, we had just been out in the clubhouse talking for a couple of hours. We came inside and I ran my hand along the back of our cream leather sofa. *Home.*

As we walked into the kitchen to make ourselves a snack, the phone rang.

"I'll get it!" SRJ jumped up and ran to the phone, grabbing it just before my mom got there.

"Oh, hello Emma," he said, handing the phone to my mom and scampering back to the living room. "It's for you, Mommy."

My mouth dropped open and I looked at Sheila. We grinned at each other. *Emma was alive!*

That night, I sat down at my computer and did a Google search for "plane crash 1985", hoping against hope not to find anything. But sure enough, the search brought up a Wikipedia entry. The crash had not been prevented. Mysteriously, the police had received an anonymous tip the night before, warning them of the disaster to come. But the future was resistant to change.

♥ March 22, 2011 ♥

Dear Diary,

So I finally finished telling you the story. But it isn't really over, is it? Sheila's coming over after school tomorrow to read the note from Grandpa Charlie with me, and we have a lot to talk about. I'm dying to know what's in it, but I don't want to read it myself.

Things with Mom have been better than usual. Somehow, when I look at her, I can't help seeing the little kid she used to be. The messy slob whose (pink!) room looked like it had been hit by a hurricane. The uncertain girl who worried her best friend would be snatched away from her, and who got bad grades in math and hated ballet. She's still on my case all the time to clean my room, brush my hair and do my homework – but something is different.

Like yesterday after school, when I was complaining I was bored, and she told me for the one millionth time that I should consider taking ballet. I looked at her and asked, "Did you like ballet when you were my age, Mom?" Usually, she just would have given me an exasperated look and told me a story about what a swell experience it was. But yesterday she just gave me a little smile, winked and said, "Well you know, my friend Marcy and I just *loved* it."

I <u>really</u> have to talk to Sheila.

A Star is
Born

♫ March 23, 2011 ♫

As soon as I woke up this morning, I could tell it was going to be one of those days. Mom came into my room with a big smile, opened the curtain to let the sun come in and started singing, "It's time to get up, it's time to get up, it's time to get up in the morning!" She was nothing if not *cheerful*.

I groaned and rolled over, pulling my blanket over my eyes. "Mom, go away!"

"Janie, you're going to be late for school again, if you don't move it!" She pulled my blanket down and stood over me, waiting patiently. "If you're late today, that'll be the third time this month. And you really should have breakfast this morning. You have your science test today, remember?" Then she turned and walked towards the door, calling out over her shoulder, "I'm going down to make breakfast, and I'm not coming up again. You're old enough to be waking up on your own."

I groaned again but sat up and rubbed my eyes. I don't think I'm much of a morning person. My parents always like to go to sleep early and wake up by 6:00. But I definitely prefer nighttime.

I trudged over to the bathroom and turned on the water in the shower, waiting for it to reach the right temperature. I always take a shower before school in the morning. RJ still takes baths, but I don't. Washing your hair in the bath is a pain.

When I got downstairs, RJ was sprawled out in front of the TV in the living room, watching Phineas and Ferb and eating a bowl of Koala Krisp cereal. SRJ!! (That means "Silly RJ", remember??)

By the way, I don't think I told you that SRJ is gluten free. He isn't exactly allergic to bread, but he has this disease called Celiac that makes it so that he can't eat wheat or regular bread or anything. He can't even have regular Cheerios! And he always has to bring his own food to birthday parties and stuff. When he was three, he used to have stomachaches all the time, and Mom and Dad took him to a lot of doctors before they finally figured out what was wrong with him. They thought I might have it too, but luckily I don't. I don't think I could *live* without regular pizza and peanut butter sandwiches.

"Mom," I said, sitting down at the table. "Why is RJ eating in front of the TV again? I thought you said we weren't allowed to do that anymore."

"Janie," she answered in her please-don't-start-with-me voice. "You're not in charge of RJ. I let him have a special treat this morning, that's all."

I rolled my eyes and snorted. "I don't think you should spoil him so much." Since there are so many things RJ's not allowed to have, he always gets tons of lollipops and special treats. My parents never let *me* have sugar cereals when I was little, but they always get RJ cool stuff like Koala Krisp, which is like chocolate Rice Krispies. And I'm never even allowed to have any, because it's so expensive.

"Janie," my mother said again, a note of warning in her voice. I opened my mouth to answer her back but saw her bite her lip and decided not to push my luck. My mom always bites her lip when she's getting mad.

It wasn't until I was halfway to school that I realized I forgot my math book at home. No matter how hard I try, I always forget stuff. Not every day, but enough so that on my last report card, Mrs. Santini wrote, *"Janie is a pleasure to have in class. She interacts very nicely with the other children and is a good friend. She's a hard worker, but she needs to work on making sure she has all her books and materials each morning."* I still remember the exact words.

If I went back home, I'd be fifteen minutes late. And then I remembered.

The medallion!

I grinned to myself and took the medallion out of my pocket. An extra fifteen minutes wouldn't be so hard to come by, after all.

******

You may have noticed that this entry didn't start with "Dear Diary." Well, when I grow up, I want to be a writer like my mom, and sometimes it's more fun just to tell the story, like a real writer would. So I'm going to do that now and again.

Anyway, I managed to get to school on time and slip into the classroom just before Mrs. Santini closed the door. I don't know how I made it through the day, though, without going completely crazy. The hours ticked by soooo slowly, I thought I was going to die! Sheila and I had been planning all week to meet in our clubhouse after school today and read Grandpa Charlie's note. I didn't want to read it without her.

As soon as the bell rang, we jumped up, grabbed our backpacks and ran to my house as fast as we could.

Once we were settled in the clubhouse with a plate of cookies and some orange juice, I took the note out of my pocket and unfolded it carefully. It was brown and faded, and the paper seemed about to crumble. It looked as if it had aged thirty years!

We sat down on the floor, and I began to read out loud to Sheila:

> *"Dear Janie,*
>
> *I don't even know where to start. Meeting you the past couple of days has been the highlight of my life. Words can't express how*

proud I am of you and of Sheila — I mean, your mom. You're a wonderful young lady, and I hope I'll get a chance to know you again in the future.

I'm deeply relieved to see that the medallion was successfully passed down to you. I'd been worried about that. It doesn't come with a manual, you know? I still don't know how it's going to happen — especially now that Ramses seems to have got hold of it. But obviously it is. And now that I know your secret language, I guess I'm going to have it engraved for you somehow, sometime in the future. All in good time, I suppose.

There is a lot I don't know, but there are a few rules that have been passed down over the generations, and this is a good opportunity for me to tell you about them.

First, the medallion may never be used to harm another human being. It must always be used for good, never for evil.

Second, the existence of the medallion must always be kept secret. Imagine what a mess our world would become if people knew that time travel was possible! Imagine what kinds of mischief could be perpetrated by unscrupulous individuals! You know, dishonest people.

Each Bearer of the Medallion may choose one person to share the secret with. Everyone else must remain ignorant! Other people who come into contact with the medallion will have no conscious memory of what they have seen. So don't bring it up with your mom — she won't have any idea what you're talking about. She may have a vague sense that things are different, or experience the occasional déjà vu, but she won't know the details.

Third, as I told you, it is incredibly important not to mess with the past. I hope everything has worked out with cousin Emma, and that my decision to intervene didn't cause more harm than good. The Law of Unintended Consequences… That being said, we are only human, and a little tinkering in extreme situations can be valuable.

And finally, being Bearer of the Medallion is a huge responsibility. For now, you don't have to worry about that. But as you get older, you'll understand what I mean. When the time is right, I have left you a key that will unlock more of the mysteries of the medallion. I put it under the loose floorboard of your mom's clubhouse, buried within the soil.

But don't go looking for it until you're ready. It will change everything.

I guess that's all for now. I love you with all my heart.

Grandpa Charlie."

When I was done reading, Sheila and I just sat there, staring at each other.

Wow. Ashideixohdi!

♫ March 30, 2011 ♫

A week has passed since we read Grandpa Charlie's note, and things have pretty much gotten back to normal. Sheila and I decided to wait a while before looking for the key. I'm not sure I'm ready. And what did Grandpa Charlie mean when he said that everything would change?

Right now I have enough to worry about.

I got to school early again today, this time without any help from the medallion. I came in and sat down at my desk, two rows behind Sheila. She was hunched over her table, scribbling furiously, so busy that she barely noticed me. I leaned forward and tried to peek over her shoulder. "What are you doing?"

"Practicing for our history quiz." Sheila always studies by copying the material over in her notebook. She says it helps her remember things. I guess it works, because she usually gets good grades.

"I already studied," I replied, taking my books out of my backpack. Have I mentioned I love history? It's one of my favorite classes. Plus, let's just say I've gotten somewhat *familiar* with the time period we've been studying — colonial America.

As I started sharpening my pencil, I heard Marcia the Snob's voice behind me. "Oh no, I touched Kellie! I touched Kellie Smelly!" I turned around to see her wiping her hand frantically on one of the coats that was hanging on the class coat rack. Kellie just sat at there, staring down at her desk. I shook my head.

Kellie Allen is a shy girl with thick brown glasses and curly, black hair. She joined our class just four months ago, right smack in the middle of fifth grade, when her family moved here from Chicago. She's really quiet and doesn't have a whole lot of friends.

No one really bothered her, until one day she made the mistake of bringing sardines for lunch. Boy, did they smell! Jeremy, a soccer nut with curly brown hair and lots of freckles, had been the first to notice.

"Kellie Smelly!" he had proclaimed, holding his nose and waving the air in front of him.

Kellie had just looked at him and gone back to eating her sandwich. But he wouldn't let up. "If you didn't smell so much, you wouldn't have to eat lunch by yourself!"

Maybe if she would have continued ignoring him, people would have forgotten about it and gone back to leaving her alone. But instead, she had replied indignantly, "I'm not by myself! I'm with three people – me, myself, and I!"

The whole class had burst into giggles, and even I had had to cover my mouth to keep from laughing. *Me, myself and I?* Could she really be that clueless?

After that, Kellie became pretty much the least popular kid in our class. Jeremy and Kenneth – another soccer nut who hung out with Jeremy all the time – started calling her "Smelly Kellie" whenever they saw her, as if it was her name. And it wasn't long before Marcia the Snob (MTS!!) and her crowd of bozos began acting as if she had the cooties, making a big fuss and wiping their hands every time they went near her. The worst was Carson, who until Kellie came along would probably have won the "least popular" contest himself. I can't stand him. He always picks his nose and wipes the boogers under his table when he thinks no one is looking. And he's mean – once I bumped into him in the hallway, and he made a terrible face at me and yelled, "Watch where you're going!" at the top of his lungs.

Anyway, Carson acts like making Kellie miserable is his personal duty. I guess he figures it'll make people forget how much they don't like him, and concentrate on Kellie instead.

I took out the rest of my books and put them in my desk, stealing glances at Kellie. She was sitting straight in her chair, concentrating on the blackboard and pretending not to have noticed what happened. That MTS is so awful! I thought. I mean, Kellie was pretty weird, and I didn't want to be her friend or anything, but that didn't mean people had to be so mean to her.

"Ok class!" my thoughts were interrupted by Mrs. Santini, who was rapping on her desk with a piece of chalk. "Quiet down, kids." She waited for the class to settle down before announcing, "Today is the day you've all been waiting for! You're going to get your science project assignments!"

A ripple of excitement went through the room. Mrs. Santini's fifth grade science projects are legendary at our school. Every year her class spends the last two months working on independent, long-term projects instead of finishing the workbook. Being in her class is considered very lucky.

"The project is going to be done in pairs," Mrs. Santini continued. "Each of you is going to work with a partner." Sheila turned around and we smiled at each other. *Of course* we were going to be together.

"But this time I don't want you working with your usual buddies," Mrs. Santini added. "I'm going to assign partners next Monday. And there will be no arguments. You get what you get, and you don't get upset. Got it?" She walked around the room, handing out the assignment sheets that explained how we would choose our projects.

A groan went through the room. Alexis, who had come in late and was just slipping into her seat, looked over at me. "Maybe we'll get to be together," she whispered.

"I hope so," I answered, happy that Alexis wanted to be with me. But I had a nagging feeling in the back of my mind. I knew I wouldn't be with Sheila, because she was definitely my "usual buddy". It seemed like Mrs. Santini wanted to mix things up a bit. I just hoped she didn't mix them up too much.

******

When I got home, my mom was working at the computer and RJ was sitting in front of the TV. He was wearing his Tweety shirt and matching shorts, and was curled up on the couch with his blanket. I walked over and gave him a hug. He could be pretty cute sometimes.

"Mom, we have to go to the mall this afternoon," I said, walking onto the kitchen and dumping my bag on the table. "I still haven't gotten a present for Alexis." Alexis invited me and Sheila to her birthday party, which is supposed to be next week. I think I'll go – at least if Sheila comes with me.

"Ok, Janie," my mom answered distractedly. "Just give me five minutes and we can go. Meanwhile, grab yourself some lunch. I made hamburgers." She gestured toward the stove, not stopping to look up from the computer. My mom is a writer and she does most of her work from home. On the one hand it's great, because it means she's home a lot and can be with us after school. A lot of my friends have babysitters and nannies and stuff. On the other hand, it seems like she's always working. When I was little we used to have "special time" every day for fifteen minutes, just the two of us. We'd take a little walk, read a story or just hang out on the porch and talk. She keeps saying she wants to go back to doing that, but somehow we always forget.

I took a hamburger and bun and sat down at the table, thinking about the science project. So I wouldn't be with Sheila, but who would I be with? I just hoped it wouldn't be Ben White. Or Jeremy. Or -

******

At the mall, I walked ahead with RJ, as my mom finished a call on her cell. She and my dad both have iphones, and my mom's totally addicted to hers. Seriously, I don't understand why she doesn't marry it if she loves it so much! She checks the news every five minutes and always has to make phone calls when we're together. I turned around and gestured impatiently. "You said you'd just be on for a minute!" I protested. "We didn't come to the mall for you to talk on your phone." A minute for my mom is like an *hour* in human time.

SRJ squeezed my hand as he skipped excitedly along next to me. "Mommy said we could get ice cream!" he said loudly, practically screaming. "I love ice cream! And this is the place that has gluten free cones!" The kid is positively *obsessed* with sweets.

As we reached the ice cream store, I spotted Alexis sitting with her mom and little brother. She was wearing her soccer uniform and eating a double scoop cone.

"Hi, Janie!" she said brightly, when she saw me. She really is a nice person. She's been really friendly ever since I got moved to her table. It's not like we're friends exactly, but I think there's definite potential. I don't see how she can stand MTS and her crowd of lousy princesses.

"Hi," I answered, getting in line with RJ. Just then, my mom turned to Alexis' mom and said, "Oh, hi Charlene! I didn't see you before. How's it going?"

"Sheila?" Alexis' mom stood up and walked over, giving my mom a hug.

"Wow, it's been a long time!"

Alexis and I exchanged glances. I had no idea our moms knew each other. How weird!

"Oh right!" my mom was saying, a wide smile on her face. "I forgot your oldest went to Middlestar Elementary with Janie." She looked at me. "Do you guys play together in school?"

"Um, actually, mom, we – um – sit together in class." I managed, looking at my feet. This was too much, even for my mom. Did we *play*? Like in the *sandbox*?

"Well that's wonderful, girls," Alexis' mom was saying. "Actually, Alexis, I would love to chat with Mrs. Ray for a few minutes. How about if you and Janie take Mitch and Janie's little brother to the play space for a little while? If that's ok with Janie's mom."

"Oh, yes, that's fine," my mom said. There's nothing she loves more than chatting with other grownups.

We paid for the ice cream and headed towards the play space, an awkward silence between us. RJ skipped ahead, happily licking his usual chocolate cone with sprinkles, while Mitch held shyly to Alexis' hand. I took careful bites of my espresso swirl, hoping that it didn't get all over my face – or worse, spill on my shirt. I'm a pretty big spiller. Luckily my hair was tied up in a scrunchie. Once I even got ice cream in my bangs and didn't notice it for hours.

"So, um, how old's Mitch?" I finally said.

"He'll be four next month," Alexis answered. Then she grinned. "He's pretty cute most of the time, but sometimes he can be a real pain in the neck. Yesterday he took my lip gloss and used it to color on the bathroom mirror! And my parents just said, 'that's not ok' and took it away from him.

He didn't even get sent to his room!"

I giggled. "That sounds just like RJ. My parents are totally soft on him. They almost never give him time outs, and they blame everything on me!"

"Tell me about it," Alexis answered. "So," she continued, changing the subject, "what do you think about the whole science project thing? What's up with Mrs. Santini saying we can't work with our friends?"

"I don't know," I bent down to wipe RJ's face and took his leftover cone as he ran off with Mitch to the play space.

"Marcia says she's not going to do the project if she doesn't get to be with me or one of her other friends," Alexis continued. I must have made a face without even realizing it, because then she said, "I know you think she's really mean and stuff. But she can be incredibly nice when she wants to. And she's super fun. Our moms are best friends from college, so we've known each other since we were babies."

I didn't say anything. I couldn't even imagine being friends with MTS. How could a nice, normal kid like Alexis be part of that crowd?

I turned around to toss RJ's cone – which by that time was dripping all over my hands – into the garbage. And it was then that I saw Kellie.

She was walking out of Irene's Music Emporium, wearing a huge yellow overcoat and large headphones. She seemed totally absorbed in whatever she was listening to and luckily didn't seem to notice us. I stood there for a moment, staring at her and wondering what she must be thinking.

Didn't she realize what a weirdo she was?

♫ April 1, 2011 ♫

Dear Diary,

Today we got back our science tests from last week, and I got an 83. Not too bad, especially considering everything that's been going on. Mrs. Santini also told us she's finished putting together the list of science project partners, but she's only going to post it on Monday afternoon. Crossing my fingers! If I were Mrs. Santini, I'd put me with Alexis, since we sit together but aren't best friends.

Today is also April Fools' Day, which in our school is kind of a big deal. Jeremy put a whoopee cushion on Mrs. Moore's chair in English class, and for once it actually worked. When she sat down, it sounded like she made the biggest fart ever. Personally, I think whoopee cushions are kind of stupid, but it was pretty funny. And the best part was, she didn't get mad at him or anything - she even laughed! I'm actually pretty surprised to find out that she has a sense of humor. Usually her face seems to be frozen in a perpetual frown. I can't remember the last time I saw her smile.

And the Sixth Grade Prank this year was *awesome*. Every year on April Fools' Day, the sixth-grade class gets to play a joke on the teachers, and sometimes even the principal. I can't wait until next year, when it'll be our turn. This year was *hysterical*! During first recess, we all suddenly heard a huge howl come from inside the teacher's lounge, and it turned out the sixth graders came in early and rearranged the teachers' cabinets. They also put a whole bag of fake cockroaches inside. And best of all, they put red food coloring in the teachers' milk, so when Mr. Johnson went to make his coffee, he thought he was pouring blood into the cup. How gross!

MTS was her usual awful self. When I went to the bathroom during lunch, she was standing in front of the mirror, brushing her hair and putting on lip gloss. As I walked by, she smirked at me. I went into the stall, closed the door and waited to see if she would leave. The last thing I needed was to have her hear me make a tinkle. She seemed to be taking her time, though, so finally I just went ahead, trying my best not to make any noise. And only when I finally heard the door open and then swing shut, did I come out to wash my hands.

In the afternoon, I found out that MTS played one of the most horrible jokes *ever* on Kellie. At lunch, I saw Alexis yell at MTS and storm out of the cafeteria, but I had no idea why. It turned out MTS had given Kellie a note on pretty pink paper first thing in the morning, telling her she was really sorry for being so mean, and inviting her to eat lunch together. But then when Kellie brought her tray to sit down next to MTS, Alexis, Jessica and that whole gang, MTS burst into laughter and said, "April Fools! Why would I want to eat with a weirdo like you?" Alexis told me Kellie just stood there, not moving all, while everybody laughed, and then she just took her tray and sat down alone at one of the other tables.

E koji TJL!!

♫ April 4, 2011 ♫

Dear Diary,

I literally think I'm going to die. Today Mrs. Santini posted the list of partners, and guess who I'm with - Kellie!!!!!

And here I was afraid I'd get stuck with Jeremy or Ben White.

The worst part is, Sheila gets to be with Alexis! They're both being super nice about it and trying not to let me see how happy they are that *they* don't have to be with Kellie, but I'm soooo jealous. It's completely unfair. And I even saw them giggling together when they thought I wasn't looking.

Jkel zioddy ljesgl!!

I went over to Sheila's after my piano lesson, so that we could talk and see if we could come up with a plan. So far – Nada. At first I thought maybe we could use the medallion to go back in time and convince Mrs. Santini to let us be together – or at least let me be with *someone* other than Kellie – but in the end I decided not to. I don't think Grandpa Charlie would have approved. And honestly, I don't think it would help. Mrs. Santini is so set on this whole "no usual buddies" idea.

I'm not sure this is a problem that even time travel can solve.

******

I was sitting on Sheila's bed, trying desperately to think of some way out of this mess, when my tablet beeped. I'm probably the only fifth grader in

Middlestar Elementary that doesn't have a cell phone. My mom says the radiation isn't good for growing kids, and she wants me to wait a couple more years before I get one. So I pretty much just use WhatsApp on my tablet. That way I can at least keep up with class messages and stuff. I don't have facebook either. My parents use it all the time, but they won't let me open an account until I'm at least 14.

My mom always used to put pictures of me on facebook, but I don't let her do that anymore. What could be more embarrassing than having hundreds of people you don't really know look at pictures of you?? Once, I was talking to Sheila on the phone in the living room, and my mom asked me to be quiet so she could concentrate on her work. I looked over her shoulder and saw she was on facebook. So I said, "What, your work's on facebook?" Then I found out she actually posted what I said in her status. How humiliating! She's promised not to do it again.

I took the tablet out of my backpack and looked at my messages. Sure enough, I had a one, but was from an unfamiliar number:

"Hi Janie, when should we meet to start working on the project?"

I looked up at Sheila. "It must be from Kellie. I never would have thought she'd have WhatsApp," I said, showing her the message. "What should I do? Should I answer her?"

"Of course you should answer her," Sheila said. "It's not like you have a choice or anything."

I pouted at her. "Well, it would be nice if you weren't trying so hard to pretend you're not happy."

"What do you mean?" Sheila protested. "Of course I'm not happy! You know I'd rather do the project with you. Why would I be happy?"

"You know what I mean. You get to be with Alexis."

"Well, that's not my fault," she said defensively. "What am I supposed to do, go around crying all day?" She stopped and took a deep breath. "Sorry. You know what I mean."

"Yeah, I know. You're right." I picked up the tablet and looked at Kellie's message again. "Should I invite her over?"

"Definitely," Sheila said. "Better do it at your house."

*****

♫ April 5, 2011 ♫

I had an even harder time than usual concentrating in school today. I kept thinking about Kellie and about what it would be like to have her come over to my house. I watched her during math class. She was wearing her huge yellow overcoat again and didn't even bother taking it off in class. And she had on these large, clunky brown shoes with pink neon shoelaces. Why did she insist on being so strange?

When the bell finally rang, I took my books out of my desk one by one, and slowly put them in my backpack. Luckily, all the things I needed were in my desk, and I wouldn't need to go to my locker. I hoped people would start going home so that nobody would see Kellie walking out with me. That was the last thing I needed. MTS and company give me enough trouble as is. Imagine what they would do if they thought I was friends with Kellie!

Kellie sat at her desk, waiting for me. When most of the kids had already gone, I zipped up my bag and walked over to her. "So, you coming?"

She nodded and stood up, looking just as awkward as I felt.

We walked in silence, Kellie a few steps behind me. We hadn't gone far, when I saw Carson approaching out of the corner of my eye. *Oh no.* I turned my face away, hoping against hope that he wouldn't see us. Or that if he did see us, he would ignore us and just keep on walking. But no — Carson is the kind of person who can't resist an opportunity to make someone else miserable.

"Kellie Smelly!" He called out in a loud, shrill voice, walking over to us. "What are you doing with Janie the Frizz? Actually," he said, smacking his forehead theatrically with his palm, "What am I saying? Of course! You're a perfect match!"

Kellie and I looked at each other, and as if by silent understanding, just kept walking without answering him.

"You guys are such chickens," he continued, stepping out in front of us to block our path. "Are you guys actually afraid to talk to me? You're scared?"

Actually, I *was* scared, but I wasn't about to let him know it. I glanced at Kellie again, and it was then that she surprised me for the first time. Without missing a beat, she stepped forward and faced Carson with her arms crossed.

"Leave. Us. Alone!" she said in a calm, but firm voice. Carson was so startled that he stumbled backwards and fell on his backside in the wet, goopy mud that had collected near the curb. He wasn't hurt or anything, but boy was he mad! She grabbed my hand and we started running as fast as we could in the direction of my house.

We came inside, huffing and puffing, and giggling as we tried to catch our breath. "Mom?" I called out.

"Yes, honey, I'm here. I'll be out in a couple of seconds. Meanwhile, you guys can take a snack."

"Ok." I grabbed a plate of cookies and we headed to the living room, where RJ was watching *High School Musical* on Netflix.

"Oh, I love that movie!" Kellie said suddenly. It was only like the second thing she had said to me since we left school.

"Me too!" I said, looking at her, surprised again. I wouldn't have pegged her as a *High School Musical* kind of girl. Actually, I wouldn't have pegged her as a normal TV kind of girl. "You want to watch for a while?"

"Sure!" she said, putting down her backpack and looking relieved. I guess I wasn't the only one who was nervous about how things were going to go. Watching TV was a good thing to do – not too much talking.

We sat and watched for a while, munching on cookies and laughing together at the funny parts. We were actually having fun! So much fun, that I kind of forgot about the science project.

As the credits came on the screen, I picked up the remote and turned off the TV.

"Hey!" RJ said, looking up at me. "Mommy said I could watch now!"

"You did watch, little guy," I told him, placing the remote on a high shelf. "You aren't supposed to watch TV all day. Mom!"

RJ pouted and got up from the couch, dragging his blanket behind him. Then he spotted the plate of cookies, which still had a couple on it.

"Hey! You have cookies!"

"They're not gluten free," I told him, picking up the plate. "Come into the kitchen and I'll give you a couple of the kind that you're allowed."

"Yay! Cookies!" He grinned broadly.

I looked over at Kellie to see how she was reacting to all this. She didn't say anything, but a small smile played on her lips.

"Do you have any brothers or sisters?" I asked her. I suddenly realized that I didn't know almost anything about her family, except that they had moved here from Chicago.

"Yeah, I have a little sister," she answered. "She's in third grade. Her name is Molly. She doesn't go to Middlestar though," Kellie continued. "She goes to Timberlake."

"Oh. Is she nice? Do you guys get along and stuff?"

"Yeah, she's ok. She's a total bookworm, though. She taught herself to read when she was like three, and she's had her nose in a book ever since. Sometimes she even walks while reading and bumps into trees and stuff." We both giggled.

"Is she as much of a cookie monster as RJ?" I asked, taking down the gluten-free chocolate-chip cookies and putting a few on a clean plate.

"Nah. Once she read a book about the evils of sugar, and she's refused to have treats ever since. Every time I have a piece of cake or chocolate or anything, she gives me a speech on how bad it is for you. It drives me crazy!"

We giggled again.

"I also have an older sister who's twenty." Kellie broke off a piece of cookie and put it in her mouth. "She's in college, in Chicago. She comes home on holidays and stuff, and sometimes on the weekends. Her name is Jackie, and she's really cool." Her face took on a wistful expression.

As Kellie was talking, I found myself wondering what would have happened if she had never brought those awful sardines for lunch. Would she have made friends by now and just become a regular person like everyone else? Would people still be so mean to her? Kellie was turning about to be a lot nicer than I had expected. And a lot funnier.

"Come on," I said, picking up my backpack and heading for the stairs. "We should probably get started on that science project."

♫ April 6, 2011 ♫

Dear Diary,

I think I'm probably the most horrible person in the world. The worst ever.

Kellie stayed over last night until eight o'clock, and I think we've come up with a great topic for our project. At first I suggested making a volcano – you know, where you make a mountain out of clay and mix baking soda, vinegar and food coloring to make an "eruption" – but Kellie said she wanted to do something more original. She's right – if we want to win, we have to come up with something really amazing. We looked on Google for a while, and came up with a really cool idea:

The Eco-Friendly Way to Empty your Flooded Basement (or as Kellie keeps calling it, EFWEFB – pronounced Ef-wef-B). Here is the description we wrote for class:

> *Did you ever wonder how it is that you can have water running out of your faucet at home, no matter whether you live at the bottom of a valley or the top of a hill? Did you ever think about how water climbs up hills – or even tall buildings – to people's sinks? It turns out that it's really a simple trick that the Romans figured out ages and ages ago. The fancy name for it is the "Communicating Vessels Principle", but it's really simple. If you have a bunch of containers that are somehow all connected, the water in each of them will always stay at the same level as the others – even if they are different sizes or shapes. The really cool thing is that this works even if what's connecting them is a pipe.*

Our plan is to build a set of Communicating Vessels and explain why they can be useful. I wish we had one last summer, when our basement flooded!

It's perfect.

While we were working together, Kellie surprised me for the third time. She started humming the tune to "When There was Me and You" from *High School Musical.* You know, the song Gabriella sings when she gets all depressed because she thinks Troy doesn't care about her. Kellie hummed it really well. It seems like she has a very nice voice.

Anyway, when I got to school this morning, Sheila ran up to me and asked how things went with Kellie last night. I looked around to make sure Kellie wasn't watching or anything, and then just shrugged my shoulders and said, "I survived". It suddenly seemed strange to be making such a big deal about it.

But when Kellie came in a few minutes later and stopped by my desk to say hello, I froze up. I just sat there like a total idiot, not answering her or anything. Sheila and Alexis were sitting right nearby, and lots of other kids were watching too. Kellie's face turned beet red, and she turned quietly away and went to sit down. For the rest of the day we just kind of ignored each other, and I sat with Sheila at lunch time as if nothing happened. Kellie ate alone at her regular table.

So that's why I'm the worst person in the entire universe. I had a good time with Kellie yesterday! So why am I too much of a coward to be her friend in school? I tried calling her this afternoon, but there was no answer at her house. I'll have to apologize to her tomorrow.

♫ April 7, 2011 ♫

Today I left the house early, hoping to catch Kellie before too many kids got to school, so I could apologize to her without everybody staring. It must have been my lucky day, because she was already there, sitting on the curb outside the school gate, and almost no one was around.

I walked over and tapped her on the shoulder. "Kellie," I began tentatively. "I'm really -"

"Janie, I don't need your favors!" Kellie stood up and whirled around to face me, her eyes on fire. "I get it! You don't want to be my friend, at least not in public!"

"No, I, uh, it's just that -"

"And I don't need your excuses, either!" She pulled her big yellow coat around her tightly and started walking away. "Do you think I'm stupid? I know why you came to apologize now, when nobody's looking. I'm good enough to be your science partner, just not good enough to be seen with! I'll come over to work on the project today after school, because I don't have any choice. But don't think I'm dying to be your friend either. You're a coward and a snob, and it's hard to think of a worse combination." And with that, she stormed off.

I stood there, for once totally and completely speechless, feeling like the biggest jerk in the entire world…

After school, when Kellie came over, things were completely weird. She didn't talk at all, except when she absolutely had to, and as soon as we were done for the day, she picked up her stuff and got ready to leave. It was awful. I was pretty quiet too, debating in my head whether to try and apologize again. Finally, just as she was walking out the door, I reached out and grabbed her shoulder.

"Kellie," I said, "please. Give me one more chance. I know you think I'm a horrible person, and I'm not proud of how I acted either. You're right, I was embarrassed to be seen with you, and I was afraid of what people would think. But that's stupid. I want to be your friend."

She turned reluctantly to face me, and I was horrified to discover that she had tears in her eyes. She was taking short, quick breaths, obviously trying hard not to cry. "It's really hard for me, ok?" she put her backpack down and sat down on the sofa. "Ever since I moved here, kids have been horrible to me. I hate this place! I want to go back to Chicago!" She sniffed.

"Yeah…" I didn't really know what to say.

"Why does everyone here have to be exactly the same, just to fit in? And were people here born in a cave? They've never heard of *sardines* before?" She had a point. Middleton is a very boring town, and people are kind of similar to one another. I mean, there are kids from many different backgrounds and stuff, but no one wants to stick out or be different. I don't consider myself to be a big conformist or anything, but even I've been bugging my parents to get me a pair of ripped jeans from Abercrombie and Fitch. Every year we get huge bags of clothes from my cousins in Cleveland, and we're usually stuck wearing them most of the time. Just our luck – they have a daughter two years older than me, and a son a year ahead of RJ. So I don't generally get new clothes. Plus, my parents think designer clothes are the stupidest thing ever. "When you have your own money, you can decide to flush it down the toilet if you want to," my dad always says, when we ask for something he thinks is outrageous.

I was quiet for a few minutes before responding. "You're right, Kellie," I said quietly. "I don't know what to say. Tomorrow I'll introduce you to Sheila and Alexis, and maybe we can all have lunch together. You want to watch some TV or something now?"

Kellie nodded, wiping her nose with a tissue. We sat down on the sofa and I flipped through the channels with the remote. There didn't seem to be anything on, except a reality show called Starbright. I'm not a huge fan of reality shows, but RJ sure is. He watches Starbright practically every Saturday night. I'm not so sure he understands it, but he loves watching the performances.

Starbright is one of those singing shows where people get up and perform in front of a bunch of judges. Then, at the end of the season, the winners of each program face off in a final contest. Whoever wins gets like a gazillion dollars and becomes really famous. Unlike a lot of other reality shows, it's actually aired live, so when people mess up, you see the whole thing. Once a girl even threw up on stage in the middle of her song, and they just kept on broadcasting, as if nothing happened. I would have died if it had been me!

Sure enough, as soon as the theme music for Starbright started playing, SRJ came running down the stairs to watch, even though he already saw the same episode on Saturday night. It's like he has a Starbright *radar* or something.

"Do you like this show?" I asked Kellie.

"Actually, I really do," she said. "I watch it most weeks. I missed it this Saturday, though."

"Ok, good." I settled back onto the sofa. It was actually kind of interesting. A group of boys from Texas, about our age, performed a rap song that wasn't too bad. And a little girl from Ohio – she couldn't have been more than five or six – sang something from Les Miserable. She was amazing, and RJ squealed with delight. I think he especially likes seeing kids his own age doing amazing stuff like that.

At one point, Kellie started singing along with the girl, and it was then I realized that she doesn't just have a *good* voice. She has an *amazing* one. She sounded like a Broadway professional! Even RJ turned around to watch her, his mouth open. When she realized we were both staring at her, she blushed and looked down.

"Wow," I said. "You really can sing!"

"Yeah, I used to get voice lessons in Chicago. We're still looking for a teacher here. I love music." I suddenly remembered seeing her in the mall, listening to her headphones and completely oblivious to what was going on around her.

After that, something weird happened. The third contestant got cold feet and refused to get on stage. They waited a few minutes, the host getting more and more excited, before announcing that members of the audience were invited to call in and take her place. The phone number of the studio flashed on the screen, and the audience went crazy, cheering and clapping. Kellie and I looked at each other.

"You should call in!" I said suddenly, jumping up from the couch. "You'd be awesome!"

"Yeah, that would be an excellent idea, if this weren't a re-run," Kellie said, laughing. I grinned sheepishly. "Anyway," she continued, "even if it were live, there would probably be a million people trying to get through to them all at once. I once spent twenty minutes trying to reach a local radio station in Chicago, when they were giving away free tee-shirts to anyone who could answer a stupid trivia question. Of course I never got through. No one ever does."

And it was then that I got the craziest, most insane idea I ever had. I nonchalantly scribbled down the phone number on the screen and pretended to laugh myself. "You're right," I said, stuffing the number into my pocket as Kellie frowned at me. "I guess you should get going now, it's nearly dinner time."

Maybe time travel *could* help solve this problem after all.

♫ April 8, 2011 ♫

Dear Diary,

Today at school I pulled Sheila aside and filled her in on what's been going on with Kellie. I told her what a good time we had after school together, and how mad she'd been when I gave her the cold shoulder the next morning. And I told her what she did to Carson, who – by the way – hasn't bothered her since. Sheila was sympathetic, but skeptical. She still thought Kellie was weird. When I introduced her to Sheila and Alexis, they went out of their way to be friendly to her, but she just clammed up and muttered barely coherent replies to everything they said. It's true they may have been faking it a bit, but they tried, and that's what counts. At lunch, I invited Kellie to come and sit with us, but she didn't want to.

After school, Sheila came over and I told her about my plan to help Kellie. She was totally flabbergasted.

"But you saw how shy she is in school," Sheila protested, when I told her what I intended to do. "How do you know she won't suddenly freeze up at just the wrong moment?"

"I don't know, I just do," I answered stubbornly. Over the past few days, I've gotten to know Kellie pretty well. She may be a lot of things, but chicken definitely isn't one of them. The girl's got guts.

I picked up my tablet and sent Kellie a message on WhatsApp: "Want to come sleep over Saturday night?" A few minutes later, the reply came: "Sure."

♫ April 9, 2011 ♫

I paced back and forth in front of our door, peeking out the window every five minutes, until Kellie's parents' car finally pulled up in front of our house. As she got out of the car, I opened the door and called out to her.

"Janie," my mom said, poking her head out from the kitchen. "What are you so nervous about? You've been acting like you're on pins and needles all evening! Is everything alright?"

I fingered the medallion in my pocket and grinned to myself. "Yeah, Mom, don't worry. Everything's fine."

"Is your friend here?" she asked. "I've made gluten free chocolate chip cookies."

"Thanks, Mom! Yeah, she's here." My mom makes the best gluten free chocolate chip cookies in the entire *universe*. They're so good, our whole family eats them instead of regular ones.

Kellie came up the walkway, dragging a pretty big suitcase behind her. Most kids just brought backpacks or plastic bags stuffed with clothes and toothbrushes to sleepovers. But Kellie had to bring a big, old suitcase. I chuckled.

After dinner we played some video games and hung out in my room for a while. Neither of us was tired. At around ten-thirty we finally got into our sleeping bags, and I closed my eyes, pretending to go to sleep. Kellie was out like a light after about five minutes. I shook her gently and whispered, "Kellie," to make sure she was really asleep. And when I saw that she was,

I grabbed some clothes, some money, my mom's iphone (I was just borrowing it, and it was for a good cause!) and a backpack, took the medallion and held Kellie's hand. "April 2, 2011! April 2, 2011! April 2, 2011!"

******

I thought Kellie must have woken up right after that, because I could hear her shrieking with me, as we fell through the tunnel. It's funny – no matter how many times I do this, I never really get used to it. It's a truly crazy feeling. Not very pleasant at all.

But when we landed in a thump in my bedroom, she was still fast asleep. I sighed with relief. This was going to be difficult enough without having to deal with all kinds of questions.

I was also relieved to see that when we landed in my room, we didn't run into some other Janie, getting ready for bed and screeching her head off at the sight of two intruders – one of them exactly like her – suddenly appearing in her room. It seems there can only be one of a person at any given time. Don't ask me why.

I looked at the clock: 8:25 p.m. Perfect!

I made sure Kellie was asleep again, and crept down the stairs to the phone, taking the crumpled phone number out of my pocket. Sure enough, RJ was curled up on the couch, watching Starbright. The little girl was just starting her song from "Les Miserable".

I reached for the phone in the living room and dialed the number, holding my breath. It was busy. I muttered under my breath and pressed redial. Still busy.

Maybe my plan wasn't all that ingenious after all. If I didn't get through in the next five minutes, it was all over.

I pressed redial another six times and got another six busy signals. Then, on my seventh try, I got a ring! I grinned to myself and gripped the phone to my ear. This just *had* to work.

The phone rang and rang, and it seemed like no one would ever pick up. "Come on!" I muttered to myself. "You gotta just pick up the - "

And it was then, just as the studio number began flashing on the screen and the audience was reacting wildly to the announcement that members of the public were invited to call in, that someone clicked on the line.

"Starbright, this is Charlene, how can I help you?"

I sighed with relief. "I have the perfect contestant for you." I said. "And we can be there in fifteen minutes."

Yeah, I forgot to tell you – The studio where Starbright is aired is right outside of Middleton, where I live. If it weren't for that piece of luck, this whole thing would hardly be possible. But if you can believe in time travel, surely you can believe in a little coincidence like that. Luck happens all the time, to all kinds of people. And Kellie definitely deserved a little luck of her own.

******

I ran upstairs and woke Kellie up, shaking her and calling her name.

"What do you want?" she protested, pulling the covers over her head. "It's the middle of the night!"

"We have to go," I insisted, dragging her to her feet. "Here, put your clothes on. I'll explain on the way." The cab I had called was already honking downstairs. "Hurry up, we need to move."

Kellie grumbled, but pulled on the clothes I gave her, grabbed her glasses, and followed me down the stairs. We were pretty much the same size – another piece of luck – so I was able to give her some of my own clothes. It was better she didn't try this with her horrible, yellow overcoat. I didn't have any shoes that would fit her, though, so she would have to wear the clunky ones with the pink shoelaces.

We got into the cab, and I gave the driver the address. I sat back in my seat and took a deep breath.

"Ok, Kellie, what songs do you know well enough to perform at a moment's notice in front of 20 million people?"

She gaped at me, her mouth open, for what seemed like five full minutes. Then she grinned and said, "Don't stop Believin', from Glee."

I grinned back at her. This was going to be *totally* awesome.

I explained to her that my dad's friend had gotten us an unexpected spot on the show, and that I had wanted to surprise her so she wouldn't be too nervous. I left out the whole time travel thing. "Obviously, if you don't want to do it, we can cancel when we get there. But if we make it in the next five minutes, they'll be holding the spot for us." I glanced nervously at the clock on the dashboard. We still had a chance of being there on time.

Kellie grinned again. She seemed more excited than nervous. "Seriously, you think I'd give up an opportunity like this?" she said. "I've been training my voice since I was like five years old. I love singing. I have terrible stage fright, but when I sing, everything somehow seems ok."

The cab pulled up in front of the studio, and we paid the driver and jumped out, running towards the entrance. A guard at the door stopped us and asked for our ID.

"We don't have any ID," I said, nervously. "I called the studio earlier, and we were told to come down here." I pointed at Kellie. "She's supposed to be a contestant on the show."

"Who did you talk to?" the guard asked, raising his eyebrow suspiciously. *Yeah, right*, he was probably thinking, *two eleven year old girls arriving at the station in the middle of the night?* What were the chances we were for real?

Oh. No. I closed my eyes and took three deep breaths, trying desperately to remember the name of the woman I had spoken to. Charlotte? No, that wasn't right. Charlie? No... And then it came to me. *Like Alexis' mom.* "Charlene!" I blurted out.

The guard dialed what must have been Charlene's number, and after talking to her for a few seconds stood aside and opened the door. "Third floor," he said, without smiling.

We ran inside and got in the elevator. I looked over at Kellie, who was still grinning from ear to ear.

And then I did the most important thing of all: I called Sheila, told her what was going on, and asked her to call all the kids in the class, starting with MTS. I wanted *everyone* to see what was going to happen.

******

When we reached the third floor, Charlene was waiting for us outside the elevator, and immediately herded us into a room across the hall.

"We have to go on in less than three minutes," she said apologetically. "And before that, I have to hear you sing. Your hair's a mess," she added frankly, "and you're not wearing any makeup. But there's nothing we can do about that now. What are you going to perform?"

Kellie cleared her throat and said softly, so that even I could barely hear her, "Don't Stop Believin'."

"What?" Charlene said, looking worried. "I didn't hear you."

Kellie cleared her throat again. "Don't Stop Believin', from Glee. Actually, by Journey, originally."

"Ok, let's hear it." Charlene looked skeptical. Actually, she had kind of a desperate look on her face, as though she was imagining what would happen if she had to tell her boss that she didn't have a contestant for him, after all.

But then Kellie started to sing. And Charlene's expression changed from one of desperation to one of astonishment.

"Ok, kid," she said, patting Kellie on the shoulder. "Get ready. You'll be on in thirty seconds."

Kellie gulped and looked at me, and I squeezed her hand. "Break a leg," I said. "Or rather, don't. You're going to be amazing."

******

I stood backstage as Kellie walked on, squinting as the bright lights hit her eyes. The studio was packed, and the audience laughed as the host announced, "Ok, things haven't exactly gone as planned this evening, but we've found a victim – I mean a contestant – who for some unknown reason was willing to come on at a moment's notice. I don't know if we'll get good singing, but at least we'll have a little comedy." Another ripple of laughter went through the crowd.

The three judges – all of them famous, although to be honest I didn't exactly know their names – were sitting in the front row, unreadable expressions on their faces. After what seemed like a long silence, the one in the middle – a cute looking guy with incredible, piercing blue eyes and an arrogant smile – spoke.

"So, you're the brave Kellie Allen," he said, looking up at Kellie, who I swear looked greener than I'd ever seen her before. "You think you can sing?" He said this with almost a sneer.

Kellie just stood there.

"I said, you think you can sing? Well," he said, turning to the audience, "I hope she can sing better than she can talk." There was more laughter. "Ok, I guess you'd better start." There was scattered applause, as the audience waited to see what would happen.

I'd forgotten how humiliating some of these reality shows can be. I swallowed, hoping I hadn't made a horrible mistake. Kellie looked back at me, and I gave her the thumbs up, trying to look more confident than I felt and thinking about all the kids in our class who were probably watching this by now on TV.

And it was then that she swallowed hard, grabbed the microphone and started to sing. After just the first few notes, the arrogant judge sat up straight in his chair, a shocked expression on his face. The other two judges were sitting forward with their mouths open, and the audience was clapping along with her singing, enraptured. Her strong, clear, beautiful voice filled the hall, even without accompaniment. She had captivated all of them. When she finished, the crowd went insanely wild. The applause and standing ovation seemed to last forever.

What happened after that was pretty weird. When Kellie came off stage there was pandemonium. People were coming over to her from all directions, trying to shake her hand and asking for her autograph. She was the program winner, of course, and she was invited back for the final contest on May 14. My mom's phone also started ringing like crazy – first Sheila, calling to let me know that *everyone* had seen Kellie's performance, and then my mom, who had been looking for her iphone, but then forgot all about it when she saw Kellie on TV. I could hear RJ squealing in the background.

We stayed at the studio until about three in the morning. There were people everywhere, and I was so tired, I could barely see straight. Finally, I was able to get Kellie alone for a second, and I held onto her arm. "This is going to seem pretty weird," I said, "but you're not really going to remember it afterwards. All I can say is -" I paused before adding quietly, "April 9, 2011! April 9, 2011! April 9, 2011!"

******

When we got back to my room, Kellie was mercifully asleep. I took the medallion out of my pocket and placed it carefully in my drawer, before getting into bed myself and dropping into a deep and much-needed sleep. I didn't know what to expect. How much would Kellie remember in the morning? And what would people be saying in school? All my thoughts jumbled together in my head as I drifted off.

♫ April 10, 2011 ♫

Dear Diary,

Luckily today was Sunday, so I had a few hours to get my head back on straight before facing what is sure to be a strange and new reality at school tomorrow. It was about ten when I felt someone shaking me and heard Kellie's excited voice in the background of my dream.

"Janie, wake up! Wake up!" She was shaking me harder. I opened one eye and then another, peering up at her and squinting at the sunlight.

"Kellie?" I sat up straight, suddenly remembering everything that had happened the night before.

"Janie, wake up! It's almost ten o'clock. Your mom is calling us down for pancakes."

I looked at her quizzically. She was acting totally normal, as if she hadn't just performed in front of twenty million people the night before. As if she hadn't just won the Starbright competition and stayed up until three in the morning signing autographs for complete strangers. And then it hit me.

We had traveled back to April 9th, 2011, *one full week* after her performance. I thought back to Grandpa Charlie's letter:

Other people who come into contact with the medallion will have no conscious memory of what they have seen.

As far as Kellie was concerned, she was sleeping over at my house a full *week* after the performance. That meant everyone had known about her leap to stardom for seven whole days.

"Um, I need to go to the bathroom." I slipped out of my sleeping bag and headed to the bathroom with my mom's iphone hidden under the elastic of my pajama pants. As soon as I was inside, I locked the door and dialed Sheila's number, breathing a sigh of relief when she answered on the first ring.

"Sheila!" I whispered into the phone, trying to keep my voice down. "I have *got* to tell you what happened last night." The story came tumbling out.

Finally, Sheila said, "I should have figured when you called me last week that time travel was involved." She obviously didn't remember anything I had told her about my plan ahead of time. There was a silence before she added, "But you've been around all week, haven't you?"

I wondered that myself. I mean, I had been around all week before using the medallion last night. But then I changed the past and never got a chance to see what happened after that. Strange. And how had I done all that without ever having started working with Kellie on the science project? I mean, she came over the first time on April 5th, but now she'd become a star on April 2nd. I shook my head. I guess that's what they mean when they talk about the "time paradox". The mind boggles.

Sheila continued, "You're so lucky you get to be with Kellie for the science project. It's not fair, you have all the luck."

I chuckled to myself. Luck, indeed.

"And guess what," Sheila was saying, "my mom finally agreed to buy me those brown shoes with pink laces everyone's wearing now. They are *so* cool."

"Brown shoes?" I asked, momentarily confused.

"You know, the ones Kellie wore for her big performance. They're the *hottest* thing now."

I chuckled again. Boy, would I have a lot of catching up to do.

******

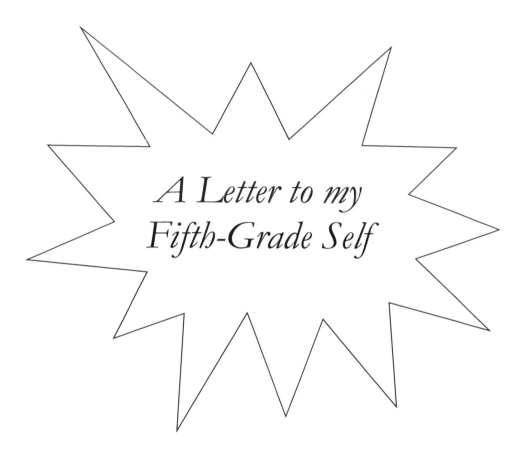

A Letter to my
Fifth-Grade Self

♫ April 11, 2011 ♫

You should have seen the look on Marcia the Snob's face when Kellie told her she wouldn't come to her stupid party this Sunday. It was *awesome*.

I was super excited to go to school today. I couldn't even sit still long enough to eat the gluten-free French toast my mom made for breakfast, and I barely managed to brush my hair and stuff it into a scrunchie before running out of the house. I just *had* to see how everyone at school was reacting to Kellie's amazing Starbright success.

I came into the classroom, trying to catch my breath from my mad dash to school, and sat down next to Alexis, who was busy writing something in her notebook with her Angry Birds pencil. I still don't get why she likes Angry Birds so much. She doesn't even have an iphone or anything to play the game on! But she's crazy about them.

I was trying to catch Kellie's eye to say hello, when MTS walked over to her and said in a loud voice, "Hi Kellie! I just *love* your coat. Where did you get it?"

Kellie was wearing the same huge, yellow overcoat she'd worn pretty much every day since she moved here from Chicago. The same huge, yellow overcoat that until last week had been mocked mercilessly by MTS and her crew of princesses.

Kellie just sat there, and the longer she ignored her, the more nervous MTS seemed to get.

"Um, maybe you'd like to come to my birthday party this Sunday afternoon?" MTS finally said, exchanging worried glances with Jessica.

Finally, Kellie looked up. "Really?" she asked. "Are you serious?"

MTS smiled broadly. "Of course I'm serious," she answered generously, gathering her long, straight brown hair into a ponytail. "It's gonna be an awesome party. We're going to decorate cupcakes, paint our nails and watch a movie! And there'll be pizza!"

Kellie didn't smile back. "I'm sorry, Marcia, I just don't think I'll be able to make it. I wouldn't want to *smell* up your house, would I? Just think how many times you'd have to wipe your hands just to get rid of my *cooties*!"

A snicker went through the room, and MTS giggled nervously. "Oh Kellie, all that stuff was just a joke! You didn't think we meant it, did you?"

Kellie just snorted in reply. MTS stood there uncertainly for a while, as if trying to think of something else she could say that would salvage her pride. Finally she turned to Jessica and said loudly, "Come on Jessica, let's go. Kellie may have a good voice, but she's still as weird as ever." The room was quiet as they headed awkwardly for their seats.

I'm pretty sure I'm not the only one who was glad to see MTS get a little taste of her own medicine.

I caught Kellie's eye and we grinned at each other. Jujil ofiluti!

******

At lunch, Kellie, Sheila and Alexis and I took our trays and sat down at a table in the corner of the cafeteria.

"Yuck, what *is* this stuff?" Sheila made a face, pushing the chicken fingers around on her plate with a fork. "The food here just seems to be getting worse and worse."

"Seriously," Alexis agreed, dumping the soft, mushy peas onto her tray. "I'm all for veggies and healthy food, but couldn't it at least be *edible*?" The school board recently decided to make our lunches more nutritious, by getting rid of some of the more obvious junk food and giving us more fruits and vegetables. Which would actually be a good idea, if the veggies they gave us weren't so *gloppy*.

"That's why I always come prepared!" Kellie said, pulling a bag of sandwiches out of her backpack. "In Chicago the cafeteria food really stunk," she explained, handing each of us a sandwich. "Sometimes I swear I could see it move!"

I giggled and accepted the sandwich she handed me, opening it up and sniffing it cautiously.

"Don't worry, no sardines today," Kellie said, raising an eyebrow. I grinned sheepishly. I actually hadn't been thinking of the sardines, but I like to know what I'm eating. Kind of a policy of mine.

"Oh, Janie always smells her sandwiches," Sheila said, taking an enormous bite of the one Kellie had given her. "Wow, yum! What is this?"

"Tuna with mayo and mustard," Kellie answered, spreading a bunch of carrot and cucumber sticks on her tray and putting it in the center of the table. "Isn't it good?"

I took a small bite of the sandwich, before opening it up and sticking a few carrot sticks inside. I like my sandwiches crunchy.

"OMG, it was awesome how you told off MTS today," Sheila was saying, her mouth full of food.

"Yeah, it was sooo -" I stopped mid-sentence. From the corner of my eye, I could see Alexis looking down uncomfortably. MTS was kind of a friend of Alexis' family, and they'd played together since they were really little.

She knew MTS had her problems, but she was still her friend, and I didn't want to make her feel bad. "Well, maybe she'll start being nicer," I finished.

"Yeah," Kellie said. "Maybe." She put her sandwich down and took a long drink of milk. "You know, Janie, I've been wondering. How were you able to get me on Starbright? How did you manage to get through to them on the phone? That's pretty incredible."

Sheila and I exchanged glances. "I, um, I guess I just got lucky."

Kellie didn't know anything about the medallion, or about how I'd taken her on a quick trip though time to the exact moment when Starbright was about to announce that one of their contestants was having a panic attack and that they were looking for a replacement from the audience. I called the studio several crucial seconds before their phone number flashed on the screen and was the first person to get through.

"Well, you're amazing," Kellie continued. "Really. After the show last week, we got tons of calls from voice teachers who want to teach me for free! It looks like I'll be starting voice lessons this week. And if I win on May 14th, I might even get to make an album!"

I smiled at her. "That's awesome, Kellie."

******

During the rest of lunch, I noticed kids stopping to stare at Kellie as they left the cafeteria. A bunch of girls were wearing clunky brown shoes with bright pink laces, like the ones Kellie usually wears, and I even spotted a few more yellow coats than usual. It's crazy how just because she's super popular now, everybody wants to copy stuff they thought was really weird before.

Just as we were about to get up, Calvin came over and sat down on the edge of the bench, right to Sheila. I thought she was going to have a heart attack. Calvin is the cutest boy in our class — he's tall, with wavy blond hair, blue eyes, and really cute dimples - and he's one of the best soccer players in our school. Sheila has had the *hugest* crush on him for, like, forever. Personally, I don't see what the big deal is. I mean, he seems like a nice kid and all. But he's just a *boy*, you know?

"You guys want to come out to a movie this weekend?" Calvin asked. Kids in our class don't really go out on dates yet - I mean, come on, we're only in fifth grade! — but there are some girls and guys who go to movies and stuff together in groups. Calvin usually goes with MTS, Jessica and those kids.

"Sure!" Sheila said right away, giving Calvin a really goofy smile.

"Great!" He grinned back at her, showing off his perfect white, straight teeth. "A group of us are going Sunday afternoon to see Never Say Never. We're meeting at the mall at two."

Sunday afternoon! So MTS and her buddies wouldn't be there. They'd be too busy with her party.

"OK," Kellie said hesitantly. "I have to check with my parents, but I think I can come."

"Me too," I said, trying to contain my excitement. This was way beyond cool. I'd never been invited to a movie group before!

"Ok." He got up and walked towards the door, smiling broadly.

"It's like being related to the queen!" I whispered to Kellie, who giggled. Then I noticed Sheila, who hadn't moved a muscle and was still sitting there, staring in Calvin's direction. I shook my head. "Hey, lovesick girl!" I tapped her on the shoulder. "Snap out of it!"

"Huh?" Sheila sat up straight and looked from me to Kellie and back again. "What?!"

"Never mind," I replied, grinning. "Let's go to English class."

******

When I got home from school, I was surprised to find the house empty. My mom and I have an arrangement – when she needs to go out in the afternoon, she leaves me a key in the huge flowerpot on our front stoop, and a note on the kitchen table. But that doesn't happen very often.

When no one answered the bell, I fished around for the key and opened the door. "Mom? RJ?" No one answered.

I walked into the kitchen, and sure enough there was a piece of paper with my name on it, held down with the salt and pepper shakers.

Dear Janie,

Sorry, I had to take RJ to the dentist for an unexpected check-up. I'll be back by 4:00 latest. I left you some spaghetti in the fridge – you can warm it up in the microwave.

Love you, Mom

I groaned, crumpling up the note and tossing it into the garbage can. I'm not sure how I feel about being left home alone in the afternoons. I like the idea of being able to be responsible for myself sometimes. After all, I'm in fifth grade! But honestly, I like it better when Mom is here. And sometimes the house seems a bit creepy when I'm alone. Not that I'm afraid of the dark or anything, like RJ is!

I heated up the spaghetti and took the plate up to my room. My parents don't love it when we eat outside of the kitchen, but if we're careful and don't make too much of a mess, they don't mind too much.

I put my stuff down and sat down at my desk. I usually try to get my homework out of the way first thing, so that I don't have it hanging over me all afternoon. I pulled out my math workbook and opened it to the page we'd been working on in class.

Fractions. UGH. I really, really hate fractions.

But only six more days until Sunday! I can't wait!

♫ April 12, 2011 ♫

Dear Diary,

ONLY FIVE MORE DAYS UNTIL SUNDAY!!

So you remember Silly RJ is gluten free, right? Anyway, it turns out that yesterday at the dentist's office, they gave him a treat for being a good boy when my mom wasn't in the room, and it had gluten in it! He got really sick and had to stay home from school today. What kind of a dentist gives a kid a chocolate chip cookie anyway? Isn't sugar supposed to be bad for your teeth?

We started going to a new dentist this year, because our old one always said things weren't going to hurt, when they did! Once I even had a baby tooth pulled, because the grown-up one had started growing in, and the baby tooth wasn't really loose yet. Our old dentist told me it wouldn't hurt at all, that it would feel just like a little pinch, but it *killed*, and I even cried a little. Our new dentist, Dr. Daring, is much nicer. But I guess if he's giving out cookies, he might be a little *too* nice.

Anyway, when I came downstairs today, SRJ was curled up in front of the TV. When he saw me, he cackled like a hyena and proclaimed in a sing-song voice, "Janie, Rainie, I don't have to go to school today, and you-u do!"

I rolled my eyes and ignored him. RJ can be *such* a pain sometimes. And if I answer him back when he's obnoxious, I'm usually the one to get in trouble. It's so unfair!!

School was pretty normal, except for the fact that Calvin, Jeremy and Kenneth sat with us at lunch, instead of with MTS and Jessica.

And Alexis, Kellie, Sheila and I spent all of math class doing Mad Libs and passing them back and forth. It was hysterical! But then Mrs. Santini caught me and Alexis giggling, and made me change back to my old seat, next to Ben White. ☹ Luckily it was just for the day.

When I got home, SRJ was sitting in front of the TV, looking pretty much the same as he had when I left for school in the morning. "Mom!" I called out, as I came inside. "Why is RJ still watching? Why do you let him watch so much TV?"

"Janie," my mom answered. "RJ has two parents. He doesn't need a third one."

"Yeah, Janie Ranie," RJ piped up from the couch.

"Mom!"

"RJ, leave your sister alone," my mom said in a tired voice. "Really, guys? Is this how we're gonna spend our afternoon?" She turned to me. "Your brother is feeling better now, I thought maybe we could work on that puzzle together."

My parents are really into family activities, like board games and puzzles and stuff. My favorite games are Monopoly and Apples to Apples. Oh, and the Settlers of Catan. I also like Rummikub. We've been working on a 1000 piece horse puzzle for about six months, but we haven't done it for a while.

"I can't, Mom," I said, "I have to call Sheila. Oh, but I wanted to ask you — Can I go to the movies on Sunday with Sheila, Kellie, Alexis and a few boys?"

My mom was quiet for a minute before answering. "I don't see why not," she finally said. Then she looked up from the computer and pulled me towards her, a wistful smile on her face. "Gosh, how time flies. I remember when you used to smear pears all over your high chair, and now you're going to movies with *boys!*"

"Mom!" I pulled away. "Why do you always have to make such a big deal about everything? It's just a group of kids!"

"I know, sweetie. It's just – you're growing up, that's all."

I made a face, but inside I felt proud. Things were changing, all right. And definitely for the better.

"Do I know these boys?" my mom was saying.

"Not really." I opened the refrigerator, took out the milk and sat down to have a bowl of Cheerios.

"Well, do they have names?"

"Yeah. Calvin Butler, Jeremy Collins, Kenny Wood and maybe one or two other kids. And Sheila, Kellie, and Alexis are coming too."

"Well, I guess it's ok, as long as the movie is appropriate. *And* as long as you finish your homework first."

"Don't worry, Mom, I will." I finished my Cheerios, put my plate and spoon in the dishwasher, grabbed the cordless phone and went upstairs to call Sheila.

♫ April 17, 2011 ♫

I think I may have gone too far. And I don't mean a little too far – I mean, *a lot* too far. Like, as in *I'm really worried something terrible will happen* too far.

Today's Sunday, so you're probably wondering how the whole movie thing went. Well, that's just the thing. First it went terribly. But then, after I went back and fixed it, it was great.

And that's exactly the problem. I don't think the medallion is supposed to be used for stuff like this. And I'm pretty sure that messing around with it against the rules can cause pretty serious trouble. So I've hidden it in my closet and have decided not to use it again, at least until I look for Grandpa Charlie's key and figure out what I'm *supposed* to do with it. And meanwhile, I'm just hoping I haven't screwed things up in any major, cosmic way.

Basically what happened was this:

The morning started out really well. As soon as I woke up I remembered: It was Sunday! I jumped out of bed and got in the shower, thinking about what I'd wear to the movie. Which is strange, because I don't usually think that much about clothes. I mean, I don't like to be a slob or anything, but I'm not a big fashion person. I usually just wear the hand-me-downs we get from our cousins in Cleveland.

After breakfast, I went back up to my room to do my math homework. Of all weekends, Mrs. Santini chose *this* one to give us ten pages of math problems, covering everything we've done since the beginning of the year. Did I mention I hate math? I sat there, trying desperately to concentrate, but I was way too excited to focus, and I kept looking at my clock, counting down the minutes until it was time to leave for the movie.

I mean, really. Would *you* be able to do math problems if you were about to go out with your first movie group??

By one o'clock I had only gotten through four problems. Or four and a half, if you counted the one I had started, but not finished. I looked at the rest of the pages and groaned – only 35 more to go.

That's one thing I *hate* about being a kid – homework on the weekends. I always have to spend at least a couple of hours on Saturday or Sunday doing homework – while my parents are doing fun stuff like working in the garden or watching a movie. SRJ always says it's not fair that I get to do all kinds of things that he isn't allowed. He doesn't realize how hard it is to be eleven, or how lucky he is not to have any responsibilities. I would love to be four again. Or at least, sometimes I feel that way.

I put my pencil down and stuffed my worksheets into my backpack. I'd just have to finish it later. I decided to shower again, just to be on the safe side, and when I was done, I even blow dried my hair so that it would be a bit straighter. Not that it made much of a difference - I still had to put it up in a ponytail. I thought wistfully of Sheila and her awesome, straight black hair that never gets messy. I would do *anything* for straight hair that behaved and didn't always frizz!!

I had decided on my one pair of fancy-ish jeans and my new pink sweater. Well, new for me anyway – it had come in the most recent bag o'clothes from my cousins in Cleveland, and still had the tags on it! My cousins buy tons of stuff and seem to throw a lot of it away before they ever have a chance to wear it. Which is kind of weird, because as far as I know, they're not rich or anything.

I pulled on my socks and looked at the clock. One twenty-five! Sheila would be here in five minutes to pick me up. I finished getting dressed and looked in my closet for my new "Teen Spirit" deodorant. It's not like I wear deodorant every day or anything, but my parents bought it for me a couple of weeks ago, and I figured today was as good a day as any to try it out.

When the doorbell rang, I came quickly down the stairs, gave my mom a quick hug and kiss and ran to the door. "You finished your homework, right Janie?" my mom called out as I stepped outside.

"Uh… yeah," I answered. I could feel my face turning red with guilt, and I regretted the words as soon as they were out of my mouth. My parents are very big on telling the truth, and they always say that trusting each other is more important than anything else. But I would *die* if I had to miss the movie. And I'd finish the math problems the second I got home. So it was kind of a white lie, right?

"Ok, honey. Just make sure to be home by four. And if you're late, don't forget to call."

"Don't worry, mom." I pulled the door shut and slipped on my jacket. It was chilly out.

"Wow, you look amazing!" I said to Sheila as we started walking towards the mall. Her hair was in a French braid and she was wearing cute, turquoise earrings. I have pierced ears, but I'm allergic to practically every kind of earring. Even gold ones bother me sometimes, so I almost never wear them.

"Thanks!" She smiled uncertainly, an uncharacteristically shy look on her face.

"Don't be so nervous. They're just boys!" That was easy for me to say. I didn't have a crush on anybody, and Sheila was about to meet up with Calvin, the boy she'd liked since practically forever.

******

When we got to the movie theater, Calvin, Kenny and Jeremy were already inside, buying popcorn with Alexis and Kellie. I looked around nervously, wondering whether any other kids from our class were going to show up. Calvin hadn't really said who else was coming, and I was relieved to see it was just them. Big groups make me kind of nervous.

Jeremy and Kenny walked over and a strong smell of aftershave filled the air. I giggled, imagining Jeremy shaving the peach fuzz on his chin. As if! If either of them shaves, I'm a monkey's uncle. They were both wearing jeans and sweaters – even Kenny, who comes to school in sweat pants or soccer shorts every single day. And Jeremy's curls seemed a little less wild than usual.

We stood there awkwardly, nobody saying anything, until Calvin walked over. "Come on, guys," he said, waving the movie tickets in front of us. "We're gonna miss the commercials."

We followed him into the theater and sat down in the third row. I got the aisle seat next to Kellie. And Sheila – trying her best to look cool and nonchalant, but blushing a lot more than usual - sat between Alexis and Calvin.

******

"That was good," I said as the lights came back on at the end of the movie.

Kellie nodded and stretched. "Yeah, not bad."

"Kind of reminds me of you," Sheila said, patting Kellie on the shoulder and giggling.

I grinned. Come to think of it, a movie about a kid who becomes a singing star *was* kind of creepily appropriate for Kellie. I mean, she isn't famous like Justin Bieber, but who knows what might happen if she wins the finals in May.

When we were outside the theater, Calvin said, "Hey, who wants to go for pizza? Carlos' is having an all-you-can-eat special."

"Oooh, I love pizza!" Sheila exclaimed, zipping up her jacket and looking at me expectantly.

"I'm up for pizza," Alexis said.

"Me, too," Kellie agreed.

I looked at the time on Sheila's phone. It was three-thirty, and I'd promised my mom I'd be home by four. I glanced at Sheila. *I guess my parents won't mind too much if I'm just a little late*, I thought to myself. After all, it wasn't every day that I was invited to go out with a whole group of kids for pizza. And I *definitely* didn't want to be the only kid who couldn't come.

"I guess I can come for a little while," I finally said.

******

Well, *a little late* might be a bit of an understatement. It was seven o'clock when I finally got home. I don't know what happened – I fully meant to stay for just a few minutes, but I was having such a good time that I totally forgot about my promise to my mom.

Carlos' pizza place was unbelievably crowded. It took us fifteen minutes just to get a table. But the food was amazing! There were seven different kinds of pizza, a salad bar and free drink refills. And a desert table that had at least ten different kinds of cookies and cakes! I'm not a huge eater, and I can't usually eat more than two pieces of pizza at a time. But I managed to have three – which was nothing compared to Kenny, Calvin and Jeremy. They must have had at least seven pieces each!

We sat around the table, joking and laughing, and I was surprised by how comfortable I felt. I never thought boys were such a big deal, but I guess I expected it to be different somehow.

"So, what did you guys think of the movie?" Calvin said through a mouthful of pizza. As he spoke, a tiny piece flew out of his mouth and landed on the table, next to Sheila's plate.

"Eeewww, that's disgusting!" Sheila shrieked, jumping up from the table. But she had a huge smile on her face. Kellie and I exchanged glances and cracked up.

"I thought it was great," Alexis said. "I kept thinking the whole time about you," she pointed at Kellie. "I mean, I know you're not Justin Bieber or anything, but you know."

"Yeah!" Sheila said, sitting back down and picking up her pizza. "And who knows – If you win on May 14th, you might become as famous as he is."

Kellie was blushing and looking down at her plate.

"I liked it too," I said, taking a sip of my drink. "I don't understand why everybody gets so excited about Justin Bieber, but the movie was cool."

It was then that I noticed Jeremy looking at me. Kind of staring, actually. I hadn't said two words to him all afternoon, and I could probably count on one hand the number of times I'd spoken to him all year. But he was looking at me in this funny way, as if he was very interested in what I was saying. I felt my cheeks turn red as I looked away.

Kellie noticed and raised an eyebrow at me. I glared at her. There was no *way* I was interested in Jeremy Collins, or any boy for that matter.

As we got up to pay, I looked at my watch and nearly fainted. It was six thirty-five! The blood drained from my face and I shoved a ten-dollar bill into Sheila's hand. "Pay for me, ok?" I grabbed my jacket, shaking, and started running for the door.

"Ok," Sheila answered. "Where -"

But I didn't wait for her reply.

******

I ran all the way home, stopping only once or twice along the way to catch my breath. My parents were going to *kill* me.

When I finally got there, I burst through the front door, totally out of breath, and called out, "Mom? Dad? I'm back!" But there was no answer.

I walked into the kitchen and put my stuff down, checking the kitchen table for a note. Nothing.

"Mom? Dad? RJ?" I called out a little louder, walking frantically towards the stairs, a note of panic creeping into my voice. I went upstairs and checked each room in the house, my heart beating in my chest. Nobody was there.

Then I heard the front door swing open.

"We gotta keep calm about this," my dad was saying.

"I know," my mom answered. "But I'm worried. Janie is a very responsible girl. She's never been this late before."

I ran down the stairs, tears welling up in my eyes. "Mom! Dad! I'm here! I'm so, so sorry!" I flung myself into my mom's arms and started crying for real.

"Janie!" My mom hugged me tightly and patted my hair. "Shh. Shh. It's ok, everything's alright."

After I calmed down, we sat down at the kitchen table to talk about what had happened. As it turned out, my parents had gone out looking for me, and must have just missed me when I ran home. They never thought of going to Carlos' Pizza, so they didn't see my friends, either.

"Janie, I'm quite frankly very surprised and disappointed," my father said. He was frowning in the way he usually does when he's upset.

"Me too, Dad. I'm really, really sorry. I don't know what happened! My friends all wanted to go out for pizza after the movie, and I thought I'd just go with them for a few minutes. I meant to come home much, much earlier. I guess I just lost track of time. I promise it won't happen again."

There was silence, before my mom said, "Ok, Janie, I think you've learned your lesson. I trust you, and I know you'll make sure to be on time next time. And if you want to stay out later, just give us a call! Who knows -" she reached out and tweaked my cheek, grinning. "We just might let you."

I smiled with relief and stood up. "I guess I'll just go finish my math homework now."

"Your math homework?" My mom asked, a puzzled look on her face. "Didn't you say you finished your homework already?"

My face turned bright red as I remembered the "little white lie" I had told my mom as I had left for the movie. I looked at her, at a loss for words. Finally, I said, "I finished some of it, but I still have some math problems that are due tomorrow."

My mom just sat there, biting her lip and staring at me, a sad look on her face. "Janie," she finally said quietly, "I'm surprised at you".

I looked down at my shoes, tears welling up in my eyes again. "I know,

Mom." I whispered. "It's just — You have no idea how badly I wanted to go that movie, and I figured I'd finish my homework as soon as I got home. I didn't mean to lie, it just kind of slipped out."

The room was so quiet you could hear a pin drop, and it seemed like hours until my dad said, "Janie, the homework isn't the issue. We could have worked something out about that. But your mom and I trust you, and we want to know that when you say something, you mean it." He leaned over and put two hands on my shoulders. "Janie, there is **nothing** more important in a family than trust. And quite frankly, your behavior today makes me wonder whether you're ready to go out to the mall on your own."

I burst into tears and pushed my chair away from the table, running upstairs to my room and slamming the door behind me.

I threw myself down on my bed and cried. If my parents had just been mad at me, I could take that. But all this *disappointment* was more than I could bear. And the worst part was —they were totally right. I hugged my pillow and cried harder. I'm not the kind of kid who usually gets into trouble, and I'm definitely not a liar. But one stupid movie group and suddenly I was acting like a stupid teenager.

I walked over to my closet and looked at myself in the mirror, wiping my eyes and staring at my puffy, tear-stained face. And it was then that I noticed the medallion sticking out from under a pile of sweaters, on the top shelf of my closet. I took in a sharp breath, reached up and pulled it down. *I could fix this.* I closed my eyes, grasped the medallion and whispered, "April 17th, 2011, 1:30 p.m. April 17th, 2011, 1:30 p.m. April 17th, 2011, 1:30 p.m."

*****

Before I knew it, I found myself back in my room, dressed and ready to go out. My hair was pulled back in a neat ponytail, and my face was clean and not at all puffy. The doorbell rang, and I ran down the stairs. This time I didn't wait for my mom to ask.

"Um, mom, about my homework…"

She looked up and raised an eyebrow. "You didn't finish it?"

"Well, it's just that Mrs. Santini gave us a huge amount of math to do this weekend, and it was really hard for me to concentrate this afternoon. I *promise* I'll do it the second I get home, ok, mom?" I held my breath, waiting for her reply.

"I guess that's ok," she said after a long pause. "I know how much you want to go to this movie. And I appreciate the fact that you told me. Just make sure to be home by four. And if you're late, don't forget to call."

"Ok mom," I said with relief, giving her an extra-hard hug. "Actually, there's a chance the kids might go for pizza after the movie. Would that be ok?"

"Sure," she said, ruffling my hair. "Just give us a call and let us know."

I had tears in my eyes as I hugged my mom again. She *was* pretty great. I thought about the messy room and frizzy hair she had when she was my age. I guess she did understand some things, after all.

******

Going through the whole movie thing again, and hearing everyone say the same things for the second time, was kind of creepy. And this time I could *definitely* tell Jeremy was staring at me. Which was both weird and annoying. Jeremy is *such* a total boy, obsessed with soccer and kind of immature. He was one of the kids who first started calling Kellie "Kellie Smelly", and even though she's decided to "forgive and forget", I still think he's kind of obnoxious.

I called my parents after the movie and told them I'd be back at seven. "Will that give you enough time to finish your math?" my mom asked.

"I think so," I answered.

"Well, seven is kind of late for a school night," she said. "I'd like you back by six-thirty."

"Ok," I said reluctantly, smiling to myself. *Parents.*

******

Things went pretty smoothly, and I'm pretty sure nothing disastrous happened as a result of my little time manipulation. But I can't get rid of the uneasy feeling that I did something wrong. Using the medallion to help Kellie was one thing — at least that was a good deed — but playing around with the past just to get myself out of trouble is probably bad karma. And I can't stop thinking about what Grandpa Charlie said about the Law of Unintended Consequences. What if something horrible happens just because of what I did? That's why I've decided not to use the medallion anymore for now.

I managed to finish my math homework, and I'm writing this with a flashlight under my covers. It's already ten o'clock, and my hand feels like it's going to fall off from writing so much. So goodnight!!

♫ April 18, 2011 ♫

Today seemed like a normal day, but I couldn't shake the sinking feeling that something was going to go wrong. And so when I got home this afternoon and found a mysterious note sticking out from under my pillow, I can't say I was all that surprised.

It was pink, with big block letters scrawled across it in black magic marker: QUZ POSEI. FOR JANIE. My heart skipped a beat as I picked it up and turned it over in my hands. It was about two pages long, and it was written in our secret language, in handwriting that was oddly familiar. I threw my bag down on my bed and down at my desk to decipher it.

******

Dear Janie,

Please don't freak out when you read this. Really. It's me – I mean you – and I couldn't think of a better way of being in touch.

I flipped it over and stared at the signature at the bottom of the page. Wzuq. Posei Zoy. A chill went up my spine and my heart started beating a little faster. *The letter was signed "Prof. Janie Ray".* I gulped and went back to deciphering it.

The year is 2030, and I'm 30 years old. Or rather – we're thirty years old. I don't want to give you too much information, and I don't want to scare you, but things have gotten pretty bad, and I need your help! I wish I could come back to talk to you, but you've probably noticed that when you go back in time, your past self

146

disappears. So the only way we can communicate is in writing.
When you're done reading this, you can answer me by leaving a
note in the back corner of the floor in your closet. I've made a tiny
hole in the wall, just big enough for a rolled-up piece of paper, and
if you put it there no one will find it. Yes, in case you're wondering,
Mom and Dad still live here!

Before I go into too much detail, please write me back, so that I
know you got this. Best to write in the secret language, so that if
anybody happens to find it, they won't know what it says.

Love,

Prof. Janie Ray

O. M. G.

I put my pen down, my hand shaking, and ran to get the phone. I seriously
needed to talk to Sheila!

******

Sheila held the letter up to the light and squinted at it.

"What are you doing?" I asked crossly. "You think I wrote it myself or
something?"

"No, of course not!" she answered quickly, putting the letter down on my
nightstand. "After everything we've been through, you really think I
wouldn't believe you?" Then she grinned. "Although technically, you kind
of did write it yourself."

I grinned back at her. "Right. So should we answer her? I mean -"

"You mean should we answer *you*?" Sheila giggled. "Yeah, let's write her back right away! It sounds like she really needs your help."

I tore a piece of paper out my yellow math notebook and started to write. "I figure I'll just make a rough draft in plain old English first, and then we can convert it into our secret language."

"Sounds good."

"What do you think of this:

> *Dear Janie,*
>
> *I can't think of anything weirder than writing letters to my older self, and I have so many questions for you!! But you probably can't answer most of them anyway. So for now - I got your letter and I'm waiting for the next one!*
>
> *Sincerely,*
>
> *Janie*"

"*Sincerely?*" Sheila looked at me and wrinkled her nose. "That sounds too formal. I mean, she *is* you after all."

I giggled, scratched out *Sincerely* and wrote *love* instead.

"Much better." Sheila said. I rolled the note up as tightly as I could and got down on my hands and knees to search for the hole in the wall. Sure enough, there it was, right behind my gray winter boots. I stuffed the note in and sat back down on my bed, looking at Sheila.

"How will we know when we get a reply?" Sheila asked.

"Good question." I got up and walked over to the closet, bending over and peeking into the hole. My note was still there. Which made sense, I guess, since it would be thirty years until my older self found it.

When I turned around to sit back down on my bed, I gasped. A new piece of pink paper with my name on it was sticking out from under my pillow!

"L-l-l-look!" I said to Sheila, picking up the note and handing it to her. "She answered already! You decipher it this time."

Sheila took the note and sat down at my desk, slowly deciphering its contents. When she was finally done, she cleared her throat and started to read aloud:

> *"Dear Janie,*
>
> *Thanks for answering me so quickly! Yes, believe me, I know how weird this is. And it's tricky, too.*
>
> *I know you haven't used Grandpa Charlie's key yet. So you don't really know that much yet about what it means to be the Bearer of the Medallion - or the Historian, as it is sometimes called. I know Grandpa Charlie told you to wait until you were ready, and I wish you could. But I desperately need your help!"*

Sheila looked up at me, a worried expression on her face. "The Historian?" she asked. "Do you know what that is?"

"No," I said softly, shaking my head. "But keep on reading!"

Sheila picked up the note and continued:

> *"As Grandpa Charlie told you, playing around with the past can be a dangerous business. I know you've done it a few times - like that time you got in trouble because you came home really late after seeing Never Say Never with your friends."*

Sheila stopped reading and raised an eyebrow at me.

"What?" I said.

"That time you saw Never Say Never? That was, like, yesterday, wasn't it?" She giggled. "Did anything happen I should know about?"

"Not really," I mumbled. I was *so* not anxious to share my little adventure from the previous day. "Just keep reading."

> *"And it doesn't seem as if any harm has been done yet, but it's best to be extremely careful.*
>
> *So I'm going to have to ask you to trust me. As the Bearer of the Medallion and the Historian, your job is to watch history as it unfolds, and help make sure it doesn't go off course. We mustn't truly interfere, of course, but we can help it along with small nudges here and there. It is our job to find the pivotal moments of history, where a tiny little change can help protect the future from disaster. And I think you are about to encounter one of those moments.*
>
> *I've been analyzing the data over and over again, and without getting into too much detail, you* must *prevent the forest fire that is going to be started during your class camping trip next month. I know you pretty well, so I know you were planning to try and get out of it, but you* have *to go and make sure the fire is put –* "

"What do you mean you weren't planning on going?" Sheila looked up from the note, giving me an indignant look. "I thought we were all going to go and have a really cool time!"

"Um…. I don't know. I was kind of hoping I could convince my parents to let me stay home. Going camping with all those kids, like MTS and company, isn't exactly what I'd call my idea of fun. But I guess now I don't really have a choice."

"Well, that's good, at least," Sheila sniffed. "I would seriously *die* if I had to go without you."

"Well, come on, keep reading."

> *"I know you pretty well, so I know you were planning to try and get out of it, but you* have *to go and make sure the fire is put out. One little forest fire may seem like not such a big deal, but according to the data I've analyzed, that fire contributed to a ripple effect, resulting in a large increase in the number of volcanic eruptions in recent years. This year several people were killed from the eruption of Mt. Sinabung in Indonesia, and if I'm right, putting out that fire could save all those lives!*
>
> *That's enough information for now. Please write me again after the trip, and let me know if everything went as planned. I know you can do this, Janie. And good luck!*
>
> *P.S. Regards to Sheila!*
>
> *Love,*
>
> *Prof. Janie Ray"*

Sheila put the note down, and we stared at each other for what seemed like hours. Things were getting very serious, *very* quickly.

******

♫ April 19, 2011 ♫

Dear Diary,

I haven't written about the class trip before, because let's just say I'm not too into it. Every year the fifth grade goes on a camping trip during the first week of May. It's kind of a tradition, and lots of kids get really excited about it. But I always figured I would try and come up with some kind of an excuse not to go. Don't get me wrong - I have nothing against sleepovers, and I like staying up all night and talking as much as the next kid. But somehow spending three days in the middle of nowhere with our whole class sounds to me like pretty much of a nightmare. Plus, I think sleeping outside is kind of creepy.

But it doesn't look like I have much of a choice now, does it?? Well, hopefully it won't be too bad, with Sheila, Alexis and Kellie there and all. And maybe we'll even hang out with Calvin, Kenneth and Jeremy. Although I've kind of been avoiding Jeremy. Even at school today he was looking at me funny.

Like in third period I went out to get a drink of water. Now that we're in fifth grade, we don't have to raise our hands to ask permission to go to the bathroom or whatever - Mrs. Santini says we're old enough to just go when we gotta go. So I went out to get a drink of water and ran into Jeremy near the boys' bathroom. Literally ran into him, that is - he wasn't looking where he was going, and he bumped into me, stepping on my foot.

"Oh! Uh... I'm so sorry!" he said, taking a step back. He was obviously really startled.

"Don't worry about it," I mumbled, looking at the floor. I was *seriously* embarrassed.

And then came the weird part. He just kept standing there, looking at me, for what seemed like forever. And then he just turned around and walked away really quickly. Boys are strange.

At lunch I sat with Sheila, because Alexis and Kellie had Classroom Duty, which means they had to straighten the classroom and stuff during lunchtime. I was kind of glad that we were alone, because we had *so* much to talk about, and we definitely couldn't say anything if Alexis and Kellie were around. Grandpa Charlie was very clear about that - I was allowed to talk to Sheila about all the time-travel stuff, but *nobody* else could know about it.

"So how do you think one little forest fire could cause volcanoes and stuff in the future?" Sheila was saying, her mouth full of mashed potatoes. Mashed potatoes seem to be the school's favorite "vegetable" these days. Not that I'm complaining - they're actually not that bad.

"I have no idea," I admitted. "Does that even make sense?"

"No clue," Sheila answered, swallowing. "I'm sure your grownup self knows what she's talking about, though. She wouldn't send you to do something like this if she didn't have a good reason."

"I guess," I said, chewing thoughtfully. "But what I don't understand is, why wouldn't the class fire be put out properly without me? I mean, we've been learning about fire safety and stuff all year long. Even dumb old Carson probably knows how to put out a fire by now!"

"Dumb old Carson?!" I swung around, horrified to see Carson standing right behind me, an unmistakable sneer on his face.

My face flushed. "Oh! Um… Carson, I…"

"Save it, nerd." Carson took a step towards me, almost touching me with his dirty cafeteria tray. He narrowed his eyes. "Stay away from me, Janie the Frizz!" he said through clenched teeth.

I stared at him, not saying anything, until he finally stepped back and started walking away. Sheila shook her head. "What a total jerk."

You guys remember Carson, right? Until Kellie came along, he was probably the least popular kid in our class, and he's really mean. When people started picking on Kellie, he seemed really relieved and went out of his way to find ways to make her miserable - until the time he tried to scare her on the way back from school and fell into the mud! After that, he left her alone. But now that kids have gone back to picking on him, he's gotten even meaner, if that's possible.

My heart was pounding and I took a deep breath. "I can't believe he heard me say that!" I whispered.

"What do you care?" Sheila said. "It's not like he's nice to kids."

"That's true, but..." I really can't stand Carson, but I do feel kind of sorry for him. I would freak out if kids picked on me the way they pick on him. Even if he *does* deserve it.

"Anyway," Sheila didn't wait for me to finish my sentence. "Forget Carson. We gotta start planning the camping trip! I soooo hope Calvin will be there."

I rolled my eyes, laughing. "Don't worry, Sheila," I said. "I have a feeling that's gonna be the least of our problems."

*****

♫ April 26, 2011 ♫

Dear Diary,

I'm really sorry I haven't written for so long. The last week has been **totally** crazy. We had three pop quizzes - one in math! (Did I mention I *hate* math??) - and I've been working really hard on a book report I have to hand in May 1st. Well, actually May 2nd, because the 1st is a Sunday. Another Sunday I'm gonna have to spend doing stupid homework, while RJ watches movies and plays with his Playmobil, and my parents do all kinds of fun stuff too. IT'S NOT FAIR!!

I really don't get why we have to have so much homework. Isn't it enough that we spend almost eight hours every day in school?? Grownups get paid when they have to work overtime, and we have to do all this work for free!! My mom says that we each have our responsibilities - she has to do her writing, Dad has to go to work (he's an electrician, by the way), and I have my school work. Only SRJ doesn't have any responsibilities yet - he's so lucky!!

For my book report I'm reading In and Out of Weeks, which was actually written by my mom. It's pretty good – and believe it or not, it's about time travel! The funny thing is, I used to hate time travel books, because they seemed so unrealistic. Pretty ironic, huh. Anyway, Mrs. Moore (our frowning English teacher, remember??) gave us a choice between two assignments: either write an essay about the main theme of the book, or make a ten-minute video clip interviewing the main character. I'm really happy I chose the video (I don't really get "themes"), but it's harder than I thought it would be.

Things at school have been pretty cool. Sheila, Kellie, Alexis and I have been hanging out together almost every day, and except for stupid Carson, nobody's called me "Janie the Frizz" in a really long time (not that I don't still hate my hair!) Even MTS has been leaving us alone, except for one little thing that happened yesterday afternoon.

It was when I was walking back from the water fountain during math class, wearing the pink sweater I told you about (the one I wore to the movies, and which has pretty much become my favorite sweater in the world these days, even though I don't really like pink so much). As soon as I saw MTS coming in the other direction, I groaned inwardly. She might not have been bothering us as much, but that didn't mean I was happy to see her.

Oh well, I thought, at least I'm dressed pretty nicely today, and even my hair is pretty much under control. I squared my shoulders and looked straight at her, determined not to be the first one to look away.

So I started to pass her, head held high, feeling more confident than usual - and blissfully, devastatingly unaware that my pink sweater wasn't exactly pink anymore. Or rather, it wasn't *only* pink. A horrifyingly huge glop of glistening, red pizza sauce had fallen on it during lunch, right smack in the middle.

MTS gave me her usual smirk. "You think you're so great, just because you're friends with Kellie now," she said, running her fingers through her long, brown hair. She was wearing a denim mini-skirt, lavender leggings, and a purple and pink top that looked like it had come off a model. She also had on matching earrings and a little golden anklet that sparkled when she walked. "Face it, Janie," she continued, "Kellie would never have become friends with you if you hadn't met her when she was the most unpopular kid in the class. And you don't seriously think she's gonna keep on hanging out with someone who wears her lunch on her shirt!" She gestured toward the front of my sweater, and when I looked down, I nearly had a heart attack. My eyes filled and I just kind of stood there, choking back tears.

"Marcia, you are such a total jerk!" I looked up and was surprised to see Kellie walking towards us. She came right up to me, put her arm around my shoulder and turned to face MTS. "Janie is one of the coolest kids in this school! You couldn't reach her level if you tried! You actually think it *matters* if someone has a stain on their shirt or can't afford all your stupid jewelry. You're such a baby, and you know *nothing* about the real world."

I have to admit, I was kind of speechless. But the best part was, MTS was speechless too. She just stood there, gaping at Kellie, and then just said "Hmph!" and walked away. It was awesome.

And to top it all off, the stain on my sweater came right off with some soap and water in the bathroom. Kellie is the greatest friend *ever*.

I really have to go now. Don't be mad if I can't write for the next few days - I have to finish all that work *and* I have to get ready for the camping trip!

♫ May 1, 2011 ♫

Dear Diary,

Today was a really fun day. I went shopping with my mom, to get the stuff I'll need for the camping trip, and we had lunch at the food court at the mall. I had sushi (vegetarian - the idea of raw fish is just too gross) and chocolate ice cream for dessert. As you know, I'm not a huge shopper, but it was fun to go to the camping store to get a sleeping bag and all that junk. I'm sharing a tent with Sheila, so I didn't have to get that.

Believe it or not, buying all that stuff for the trip (we're leaving tomorrow!!) actually made me get a bit excited about it. Well, excited might be a bit of an exaggeration. Let's just say I'm not dreading it quite as much as I was before. Kind of of like how buying school supplies makes you a little bit excited about starting the new year, even if you really don't want the summer to end.

RJ wanted to come with us, but Mom made him stay home with Dad. She says its important for each of us to have "special time" alone with our parents. I think she's definitely right about that. I feel like I never get to talk with my parents anymore, with RJ butting in and demanding all the attention. Anyway, she promised to bring him back a gluten-free ice cream cone, so he wasn't too upset.

I gotta go pack now. The bus is leaving at 7:00 tomorrow morning!

♫ May 4, 2011 ♫

Dear Diary,

As soon as I opened the front door tonight and lugged my backpack through the entrance, my parents jumped up and ran over to me.

"Janie!" My mom wrapped her arms around me and squeezed, a little too tightly. "We missed you! Mrs. Santini told us what happened on your trip. Are you ok?"

I hugged her back. "Yeah, Mom, don't worry. Everything's fine now." I sure was glad to be home.

My dad reached over and gave me a kiss. "Sounds like you had more excitement than you bargained for! Mrs. Santini said if it hadn't been for you, things might have turned out a whole lot worse. We're proud of you, honey."

I smiled at him as I put my backpack down on the banister, stretching my arms. My back was sorer than I had realized.

"Well, come sit down with us in the kitchen and tell us the whole story! Your mom made you a cup of tea and your favorite blueberry muffins."

"With gluten?" Now that RJ is gluten free, my mom almost never makes regular desserts anymore.

She nodded. "With gluten."

"Thanks guys! Um, I really want to tell you everything, but first I need to go upstairs and, um, go to the bathroom."

Without waiting for a reply, I raced up the stairs and into my room. Sure enough, a little pink note with "QUZ POSEI" scrawled across it was sticking out of my pillow. I grabbed it and opened it up, not daring to breathe. "NUUM PUH."

I sighed and stuffed it back under my pillow, before slowly walking back downstairs and sitting down at the kitchen table to tell my parents the whole story…

******

It was 7:25 by the time the bus actually came, and as I climbed the stairs with my backpack - it was heavier than I had thought it would be! - I heard Sheila and Kellie calling out to me, "Janie, come sit with us, we saved you a seat!" I grinned back at them and waved as I surveyed the bus. It was already full - mine had been the last stop.

"Come on Janie, go sit down. so we can get going!" Mr. Brandish, the bus driver, interrupted my thoughts. He sounded harsh but was smiling broadly. He was pretty nice most of the time.

I smiled back and lugged my backpack towards the back of the bus where my friends were waiting. After I sat down next to Alexis, every single seat was taken. Except, that is, for the one right next to Carson, who was sitting right in front of us. *Nobody* wanted to sit there.

The twinge of pity I felt for him disappeared almost immediately, when he turned around and caught my gaze. "What ya staring at, Janie the Frizz?" he said with a smirk. I looked away quickly and turned my attention back to my friends.

"What do you have in that backpack, Janie?" Sheila was saying. "I hope you didn't bring too much stuff. We're gonna have to carry our bags for *hours*."

"I don't know," I said defensively. I didn't think I brought anything extra, but maybe I had gotten a little carried away, with all that shopping we did.

"Well, there's nothing you can do about it now," Sheila said. She was nothing if not *direct*.

"Hey, look what I brought," Kellie said, changing the subject. She stretched out her hand and offered us some of the homemade chocolate-chip cookies her dad likes to make.

"Yum." I forgot all about my heavy bag.

"I'm so excited!" Alexis squealed, jumping up and down in her seat and taking a bite of a cookie. "We're gonna stay up all night and talk and eat cookies and marshmallows! This is going to be amazing!"

Sheila and I exchanged glances. I sure hoped she was right.

******

By the time we reached Quickstone National Park, half the kids on the bus were asleep, and the other half were singing "99 Bottles of Beer on the Wall." Even Mrs. Santini. I guess she figured - if you can't beat 'em, join 'em. Actually, she seemed like she was having a good time. Even Mrs. Moore was smiling.

Mrs. Santini stood as we pulled into a parking lot surrounded by ginormous pine trees. "All right, kids, up and at 'em, we're here! Jeremy," she pointed at Jeremy who was leaning sleepily against the wall of the bus, "you grab the water bottles with Calvin. And Alexis, Sheila, Kellie and Janie," she turned to face us, "you guys take the snacks. And don't worry," she added, before we could groan, "We're going to switch off."

We grabbed the stuff and started walking. "We're going to walk for about 45 minutes," Mrs. Santini announced, "and then we'll break for snack. I want you guys to pair up in buddies, and I'm going to give each of you a number. That way we'll make sure nobody gets lost. And no wandering off! We need to stick together."

I paired off with Sheila, and Kellie was with Alexis. It didn't matter, though - we were all going to be together anyway.

"Carson, I said to choose a buddy," Mrs. Santini was frowning at Carson, who was standing alone on the side of the path.

"I, um…" His voice trailed off. "I, um, kind of don't have a stupid buddy." There were more than a few snickers.

"Carson! We do not say -" Mrs. Santini stopped suddenly and smacked her forehead. "Oh, right, I forgot that Andy is sick today and so we're an odd number! I'm so sorry, Carson, you can be my buddy."

Carson hung his head and didn't say anything. If you ask me, he looked like he wanted to disappear.

It was five o'clock before we reached the clearing where we planned to set up camp, and I was e-x-h-a-u-s-t-e-d. Did I mention I was tired? By then we had stopped for two snack breaks, one lunch break, and a really cool swim in a stream that passes through the park. The water was freezing (it is only May, after all), but that didn't stop most of the kids from going in. Even Sheila and Alexis did. Kellie and I just kind of sat on the side and put our feet in. For one thing, I really don't like my bathing suit, and the last thing I need is for the whole class to see me in it. It's kind of babyish, and even though my mom promised me we'd get a new one this summer, we haven't yet. And for another thing, being really, really cold and wet isn't exactly my idea of a good time.

For some reason, as I sat there, I had a sudden image of RJ jumping into the water and giggling, and for just about a split second I realized I missed him. He could be a pain, but he was a cute a little guy. I guess absence makes the heart grow fonder.

The first night was pretty uneventful. We pitched our tents, made dinner and started a campfire. It was really fun. We roasted about a million marshmallows, and it turned out Mrs. Moore brought chocolate and graham crackers as a surprise, so we could make s'mores. They were really good! Before we finally went to bed at around midnight, I made absolutely sure the fire was out, and wondered to myself why the older Janie (kind of weird to think about her, I mean me, as a separate person) thought they needed me for that. Everyone seemed to know how to put out the fire, and they were doing just fine without me.

I fell asleep pretty much the second my head hit the pillow, and the next thing I knew, Sheila was pulling on my arm and whispering, "Janie, come on! It's time to get up! If you don't hurry, you'll miss breakfast!"

I groaned and rolled over, pulling the sleeping bag over my head.

"Go 'way."

"Janie, come on!" Sheila shook me gently, but sounded impatient.

I sat up slowly and groaned again. My mouth felt pasty and my eyes were full of sleep. And I suddenly realized that I really, really had to go to the bathroom. I struggled to my feet and looked at Sheila, who was already dressed in cut-off shorts and a green tee-shirt. She looked positively *cheerful*.

"Um… Will you come with me to the bathroom?" If there was one thing I dreaded, it was going to the disgusting outhouse and the outdoor sink we shared with all the girls in the class on my own. Letting everyone see me before I could even wash my hair and brush my teeth would be bad enough when we were together.

"Sure. I also need to brush my teeth. But we should hurry. Mrs. Santini said we need to leave by nine."

Nine? How late had I slept? I peered down at my watch. It was 8:35.

******

The rest of the day was pretty uneventful too, and I had almost forgotten about the whole fire thing. We hiked, made homemade pita bread and chamomile tea for lunch, and spent the afternoon resting near the campsite. I couldn't believe I had almost decided to stay home! I guess it was lucky I had gotten that note from myself, and not only so that I could help fix history.

"Ok, I have the funniest joke ever," Kellie said, popping another piece of caramel popcorn into her mouth. We were sitting around her and Alexis' tent, eating junk food and cracking up about pretty much nothing. And boy, did she come prepared - popcorn, Doritos, potato chips, mint-chocolate chips. Yum. "A woman goes into her bathroom, and is shocked to find an elephant in her bathtub. She asks the elephant, 'What are you doing in my bathtub?' And the elephant says…"

She looked up at us to make sure she had our full attention and said dramatically, 'No soap radio!" Then she burst into wild giggles. Sheila, Alexis and I just stared at her.

Kellie stopped laughing as quickly as she had started. "You guys passed the test!" she said triumphantly, as we looked at each other quizzically.

Sheila leaned over and stage-whispered in my ear, "I think she's finally lost it."

Kellie laughed again. "No, see, that's not a real joke. It's a test to see if you're a conformist."

"A conformist?" I asked.

"Yeah, like if you just do things because everybody else is doing them. The joke isn't really funny, it doesn't really mean anything. And the person who tells it is just supposed to laugh to see if the people listening will laugh too. You know, so that nobody can tell they don't really get it. At my old school pretty much everybody would have laughed. But you didn't." Her voice suddenly became serious. "And that's why I like you guys so much. You're *real*."

I shivered slightly and pulled my sweater more tightly around my shoulders. Despite the cool afternoon air, I felt a warm glow inside. These guys truly were my *friends*.

I was shaken out of my thoughts by a scream on the other side of the campsite. "No, that's mine!" Carson was yelling, as he chased after another boy. The boy started running but then thought better of it and stopped, tossing something at Carson. "Fine, be a baby if you want it so badly," he said. "It's just a stupid lighter."

I shook my head as I watched. That Carson sure was messed up.

******

It was after dinner that I noticed Mrs. Santini standing in the corner, whispering something nervously to Ms. Moore. They both looked worried.

"Well, when did you notice he was gone?" Mrs. Moore was saying, trying to keep her voice down.

"Just a few minutes ago. But come to think of it, I don't remember seeing him during dinner. He probably just went to the bathroom. If it were anyone else, I wouldn't be so concerned. But you know…." Her voice trailed off.

I looked around, wondering who they were talking about. Just then I saw Alexis and Sheila, who were coming back from the bathroom.

"Hey, did you guys happen to see anyone around the boys' outhouse?" I asked them.

"No," Alexis said, putting her wash bag down next to her tent. "And they were both open. I grabbed a tissue from the girls' outhouse, and the boys' outhouse… Well, let's just say it didn't look like anyone could use it." She wrinkled her nose at the thought.

"What she means is, it was open and there was dirty toilet paper stuffed into the toilet," Sheila said, rolling her eyes. Sheila isn't one to beat around the bush.

I shifted my weight nervously. "I overheard Mrs. Santini saying someone was missing, and that they might be in the bathroom. I guess I should go tell her it was empty."

I walked over to Mrs. Santini and Mrs Moore and told them about the bathroom.

"Ok, thank you sweetie," Mrs. Santini patted my head, but she was looking at Mrs. Moore, her expression even more worried than before.

"Um, well, who is it that's missing?" I asked nervously. "Maybe me and some other kids could start looking for them."

"Oh don't worry yourself about it," Mrs. Santini tried to suppress the panic in her voice. "I wish you hadn't overheard our conversation. I'm sure Carson will show up soon. You go ahead and let us grownups take care of this."

So it *was* Carson. It *so* figured he would be the one to run off and cause trouble. But as I turned away, something was bothering me. A thought that I couldn't quite put my finger on. There was something…

Five minutes later, after I made sure the campfire was out and got ready to put on my pajamas, I froze. It hit me like a bucket of freezing water being splashed in my face. *Carson had a lighter.*

I rushed over to Mrs. Santini, my throat tight with fear. We didn't have a minute to lose.

******

"Janie, I understand what you're saying," Mrs. Santini said. "But I've called the park rangers and the police, and they're coming out to look for him. They'll be here in a few minutes, and they specifically said we should wait here. The last thing they need is for us *all* to go missing."

"But Mrs. Santini," I protested. "The park rangers don't know that he has a lighter and that he's going to start a fire!"

Mrs. Santini stared at me, an odd look in her eyes. "Sweetie, I know you want to help, but you can't possibly know he's planning to start a fire."

My face flushed, and I thought back to the little "white lie" I had told my parents, and all the trouble it had caused. But this was different, wasn't it? This was to help somebody. "I, uh, I heard him say he was going to start a fire," I said, trying to keep my voice steady. "I didn't think he really meant it, but now that he's missing… I really think that's what he's going to do." I swallowed hard. *I'd better be right.*

Jeremy, who had been listening closely to our conversation, suddenly spoke up. "I think Janie's right, Mrs. Santini," he said urgently. "And I think I even know where he might be. We saw a cave about ten minutes down that way," he gestured toward the path we had come on, "and he seemed really excited about it." Jeremy looked over at me and grinned, and I smiled back gratefully.

******

Mrs. Santini didn't need much convincing after that. We paired up into buddies, filled as many water bottles as we could, and headed off in the direction of the cave. Mrs. Santini called the rangers to let them know where we were going, just to be on the safe side.

Sure enough, as we approached the cave, the smell of smoke became overwhelming. And as we got even closer, we could hear the sound of crying coming from inside the cave. The entrance to the cave seemed to be blocked by the fire, and Carson was trapped inside!

"Oh my goodness!" Mrs. Santini pulled out her phone again to call the rangers. "Ok, everyone," her voice was shaking. "Don't go near the fire, just hand me your water bottles, one by one." And slowly but surely, the fire sizzled out as she poured the water over it. Luckily, the wind blew the smoke away from the cave, and it wasn't long before Carson could come out. By the time the rangers arrived, Carson was sitting on the ground next to Mrs. Santini, wrapped in a blanket and sipping cold tea with sugar.

"You know you broke a lot of rules, Carson, and we're going to have to have a serious talk about that later," Mrs. Santini said in a soft but serious voice, putting her arm around Carson's shoulder. "But for now - you should just know how lucky you are. If it hadn't been for Janie and Jeremy here, it might have taken us a whole lot longer to find you!"

Carson looked up at me then, a strange expression on his face. If I didn't know better, I'd have sworn it was gratitude. "I – I – I was just trying to see how long it would take for a leaf to catch fire," he managed. "I didn't...think-"

He sure didn't.

Before we left to head back to our campsite, I made sure the fire was totally out. I wasn't going to take any chances. By then it was close to one in the morning, and everyone was pretty pooped.

The ride back home was pretty much like the ride there, with one big exception. After Carson sat down and put his backpack on the seat next to him, Jeremy came up with his hands on his hips and said in a loud voice, "Carson, it really isn't nice to take up two seats like that. Come on, move your backpack! I wanna sit down already!"

Carson looked like his eyes were gonna pop right out of his head. He picked up his backpack and muttered, "Fine, have it your way," in his usual surly tone. But I'll be a monkey's uncle if there wasn't just the teeniest smile on his face.

I sat back in my seat and yawned, getting ready to sleep during the ride home. *Hmmm* I thought vaguely as I drifted off. *Maybe Jeremy was kind of cute after all.*

******

So that's the story. And now you can see why I was so relieved to find a note on my pillow from Prof. Janie Ray (yup, that's me), saying "Good job".

I know things aren't just going to go back to normal, but that's OK. Sheila and I are planning to look for Grandpa Charlie's key after school tomorrow, and then we'll know exactly what "secrets" he was talking about. Kellie is going back to Starbright for the final Showdown in less than two weeks!! And I think I'm beginning to see that change isn't always a bad thing.

But for now, I guess, it's just good night.

Baking with Frenemies!

♥ May 6, 2011 ♥

Dear Diary,

You are NOT going to believe this. Granted, I've asked you to believe a lot of pretty impossible and strange things over the past few weeks. But this is even weirder. It goes against *nature*, like dropping a ball and having it fall *up* rather than down. Or putting something in the freezer and having it get really hot.

Or – well, I think you get the idea.

Remember MTS, AKA Marcia the Snob? The most "popular" and annoying person in our whole school, who started the whole "Janie the Frizz" thing and used to pick on Kellie *every day*?? Well, it turns out she wants to be our friend!!! Alexis told me Marcia's been begging her to let her sit with us at lunch and to invite her to our next movie group. Which is really, really crazy. Before all this *stuff* started happening, if we went anywhere *near* Marcia's table, she'd give us the evil eye and say really horrible things to us.

Alexis, who's been friends with Marcia since they were little (their moms went to college together, so they didn't really have a choice), says that MTS can be really nice sometimes, and that we should give her a chance. But I'm not so sure. MTS has always gone out of her way to make me feel excluded, and when Kellie first came to Middlestar Elementary School, she was perfectly *awful* to her. She acted like Kellie had the cooties!

And remember the April Fools "joke"?

Just when Kellie was feeling the loneliest, Marcia gave her a note telling her she was really sorry for being such a jerk and inviting her to eat lunch with her friends. But when Kellie showed up in the cafeteria and came to sit down at MTS' table, Marcia and her stupid friends all laughed at her and said, "April Fools! Why would we want to eat with a weirdo like you?" Kellie was horrified and even Alexis stopped talking to Marcia for like a week. Have you ever heard of anyone being so unbelievably nasty and cruel? Who does things like that?? Alexis says that Marcia acts that way because she's kind of insecure. But I'm not sure I believe that. Marcia seems to have plenty of self-confidence, and she's got tons of friends. If anything, she's not insecure enough!!

Anyway, Sheila, Alexis and Kellie are coming over tomorrow morning to talk about the whole MTS situation and decide what to do. Personally, I think if we are going to let her be our friend, we first have to make sure that she's for real. She probably just wants to be friends now because of Kellie, and because a lot of kids have started hanging out with us these days.

Oh, and I almost forgot! You're probably wondering what happened when Sheila and I met after school today to look for Grandpa Charlie's secret key. But she didn't end up coming over, because at the last minute her mom told her she had to babysit for her little cousin Gertie, who's visiting from Missouri. So instead, I went over to her house, and we made mint chocolate chip cookies, to practice for the baking contest we're having at school next Wednesday. Every year the fifth grade has a baking contest to raise money for a different charity. The winner gets a 20$ gift certificate to Absolutely Muffins, which is only the greatest bakery in town, and right down the street from our school. This year we're raising money for UNICEF.

Anyway, the cookies were amazing!! I never knew how easy it was to make mint flavored things – you just have to put a few drops of mint extract into the batter. YUM! We decorated the cookies with royal icing in all different colors and sprinkles and stuff. And we made special ones for Alexis and

Kellie, to surprise them with tomorrow – an Angry Birds one for Alexis (of course!) and one shaped like a musical note for Kellie.

Gertie mixed all the ingredients together and helped with the decorations. She's one of the cutest little kids I've ever seen!! Even though she's only three years old, she almost never cries and when she smiles, she has these adorable little dimples on her cheeks. She loves purple, so we mixed red and blue together to make purple royal icing, which for some reason made her giggle like crazy. And she has this little doll she takes with her everywhere she goes. I wish RJ could be more like Gertie, and less of a pain!!

Gertie's mom is kind of sick, and they came out here for a doctor's appointment or something. Sheila doesn't know exactly what's going on (her parents are pretty big on privacy), but it must be pretty serious for them to come all the way out here just to see a doctor. I can't even imagine what it's like for Gertie to have a sick mom - I'd be so worried all the time if I was her!

Luckily, I guess she's too little to really understand what's going on, although I think even little kids usually know when something's wrong, even if the grown-ups don't think they do. I remember when I was in first grade, my dad got fired from his job. I woke up one morning and found him in the kitchen making this huge breakfast for me and my mom – pancakes, French toast, and everything. He gave me a big smile and told me that he was on vacation from work, and I jumped up and down and squealed with excitement. For a few weeks he was around every morning, and I was so happy – but slowly I began to realize that even though my parents were pretending everything was great, they were really worried. One night I couldn't fall asleep, and I heard them yelling at each other about money in the living room. They don't fight very often, but when they do, they yell a lot. When I asked them if it meant we were poor, they told me I was being silly and acted as if they didn't know what I was talking about. But I knew something was wrong, and it made me so mad that they wouldn't admit it!! I hate it when grown-ups think kids are stupid, just because they're smaller. I really hope Gertie's mom will be ok!

♥ May 7, 2011 ♥

"Oh my gosh, these are amazing!" Kellie pushed her curly, black bangs away from her eyes and held her cookie out in front of her, peering over her glasses to inspect it. "You guys'll win the baking contest for sure!"

"Thanks!" Sheila said, smiling proudly. "Janie and I made them yesterday while I was babysitting for Gertie. We thought you guys would like them."

"Even I've never had an Angry Birds cookie," Alexis said, giggling. "This looks almost too good to eat!" She placed her cookie on a plastic plate on the floor of the clubhouse and plopped down on the red poof my parents gave me last year for Christmas.

"I don't know," Kellie said, taking a huge bite of her cookie and shaking her head with mock disapproval. "I've never heard of a cookie that was too good to eat!"

We all laughed, sitting down next to Alexis. Sheila reached over to turn on the fan we had finally managed to set up in the clubhouse. It was an unusually hot day for May, and even though we were all wearing shorts and short sleeves, we were sweating like crazy. The windows of the clubhouse were all open, but the air was humid and sticky and the room still felt stuffy.

"Ahh, that feels good!" Sheila said, putting her face right up in front of the fan and letting it blow back her straight black hair.

"Hey, move it!" I said grumpily, pulling Sheila over to the side. "Don't hog the fan!"

"Geez, you don't have to be so – "

"Guys, come on, stop it. We're here to talk about Marcia, right? Not to fight over silly stuff." Alexis' face was serious. "Let's put on some music. Simon and Garfunkle? The Beatles?" Ever since Sheila and I got back from our little trip to 1985, we'd been into The Beatles, which as it turned out was one of my mom's favorite bands when she was my age. And even though Alexis and Kellie hadn't been with us –and come to think of it, didn't know anything about the medallion - our sudden interest in all things retro seemed to be wearing off on them.

"How about 'Help'?" I suggested, leaning over and plugging my ipod into the speakers.

Kellie groaned. "I'm the last person to question unusual taste in music," she said. "And I do like 60s stuff, really. But does it have to be all retro all the time?? How about some Lady Gaga? Or 1D?"

"Ok, fine." I flipped through the songs on my ipod until reaching "Born this Way". "How about this? Actually, this song may be good background music for talking about Marcia, and her – um – lack of ability to accept people as they are. It wouldn't kill her to listen to it herself!"

"Seriously," Sheila snorted. "She's a bully."

"Look, I've been friends with Marcia for a really long time," Alexis said, looking uncomfortable. "And I know how mean she can be. But here you guys are talking about how important it is to accept other people as they are, and you're not even willing to give her a chance!"

"A chance?" I said, gesturing towards Kellie. "Do you remember how horrible she was to Kellie when she first got here? No offence, Kellie, but if you hadn't won the Starbright competition, Marcia would never want to be our friend."

"I'm not offended, I think you're right," Kellie said quietly. "But..." Kellie's voice trailed off.

"But what?" Sheila and I said at the same time. We looked at each other. "Jinx, buy me a coke," I said, laughing.

Kellie stared at the floor, looking uncomfortable. Finally she said, "Well, it's just that... You know, she wasn't exactly the only one who was mean to me."

Sheila and I exchanged embarrassed glances. Kellie definitely had a point. Jeremy and Kenny, who had been hanging out with us the past few weeks, had been the first ones to start calling her "Kellie Smelly", and even I had taken a few days to admit to becoming her friend. She had forgiven us, so maybe we should be willing to forgive Marcia, too.

"Well, how can we make sure this isn't one of Marcia's little tricks?" Sheila asked, taking a cookie out of the box and stuffing it into her mouth. "I'd be willing to give her a chance if I thought she meant it. Is there some way we can test her or something? Find out what she's really up to?"

There was quiet for several seconds, before I jumped up, nearly spilling Alexis' water bottle. "I've got it!" I said excitedly.

"By George, she's got it!" Kellie said in a fake British accent, giggling.

"Is it contagious?" Sheila made a funny face at me and I groaned and pelted her with cookie crumbs, rolling my eyes.

"I know how we can test Marcia to see if she's really changed!" I was talking quickly, the words tumbling out. "Kellie and I will pretend to have a big fight, a really nasty one. We'll convince Marcia we're really mad at each other. And then Kellie can ask Marcia to be her baking contest partner and try and convince her to mess up our recipe by, like, changing around the salt and sugar or something. If Marcia agrees to go along with it, we'll know she's still her scheming, obnoxious self. But if she refuses, we'll know we can trust her. What do you guys think?"

"I don't know," Sheila said thoughtfully. "Lots of kids might agree to go along with a prank like that. Even if they're not super mean. They might just think it's funny."

"I guess." Although it did seem kind of mean to me. I sat back down.

Then Sheila exclaimed, "I know!" We all looked at her. "You'll have the fight with Kellie, and when she thinks you're really mad at each other, Kellie will let it slip that you're hiding your secret cookie recipe for the contest in your diary. And she'll try and convince her to steal it out of your bag!"

"My diary?!" I shrieked. "No way!" I was shaking my head vehemently. "Never!"

"We won't use your real diary, silly. It'll be a fake one. And when Marcia opens it up, she'll find a note from us telling her what a jerk she is and why we can never trust her. If she doesn't open it – we'll know she's changed."

Alexis was staring at us, her mouth open, slowly shaking her head. "I don't know, Sheila, that sounds kind of.."

"Yeah, it's kind of mean," Sheila interrupted, "but we have to do *something* to see if Marcia's changed. It's not our fault she's been so awful for so many years. And anyway, if she has changed, she'll never see the inside of the diary anyway." She turned to Kellie. "Kellie, what do you think? Do you think you can pull it off?"

Kellie raised an eyebrow and grinned. "Yup. I can do it. I have lessons all week for the Starbright Showdown next Saturday, but I'll be at school at least until Wednesday." The Starbright finals were just a week away (!) and Kellie was spending almost all her spare time preparing.

I pushed away the uneasy feeling in my stomach and nodded my head. "OK, so it's settled! But what will our 'fight' be about?"

"Um.. I don't know. Maybe you can pretend you're angry at me for being obsessed with the Starbright competition and acting stuck up?" I nodded. Actually, it was kind of amazing that Kellie *hadn't* been more obsessed and stuck up and was still acting like a normal kid. Well, normal for Kellie anyway.

"Sounds good. So we'll have our first big argument Monday morning in English?"

"Sure." Kellie grinned again and stood up, brushing the crumbs off her jeans and grabbing the big yellow coat she still couldn't seem to get enough of. "I gotta go, though, guys. I've got a voice lesson in twenty minutes."

It was only after I got up too that I noticed that Alexis was still sitting there, shaking her head and looking down at the floor. And then, without saying a word, she got up and left.

♥ May 9, 2011 ♥

Dear Diary,

When I got to school this morning, I put my backpack down on my desk and looked around. Luckily, I had managed to get there early and the classroom was pretty empty. I looked at the clock: 7:45. I really hoped Kellie got there early enough so that we could talk before staging our big fight, and I was nervous about seeing Marcia. I'm not exactly the greatest actress in the world, and I was worried MTS would see right through me. I had tried calling Kellie after our meeting yesterday, but her mom said she was in the middle of a voice lesson and couldn't come to the phone. And I *definitely* didn't want to bother her while she was rehearsing for Starbright. That one performance could change her whole life!

Finally, after what seemed like hours, Kellie walked in. By then lots of kids had gotten to school, but I was relieved to see that Marcia hadn't come in yet. Trying to look nonchalant, I caught Kellie's eye. She looked just as nervous as I was.

I made a slight motion with my head, trying to indicate we should go out and talk in the hallway, without being too obvious about it. Kellie nodded, and I got up and walked out of the classroom. In the bathroom, I checked the stalls to make sure nobody was inside. Thankfully, it was empty.

Kellie followed me inside, and as soon as the door closed behind her we burst into laughter.

"This is ridiculous!" she sputtered between giggles. "You're acting like we're in some kind of a spy novel."

"I know," I said, taking deep breaths to try and stop laughing. "I guess I'm just… I don't know. It really isn't such a big deal."

"Yeah. Ok. So you go back in first, and I'll follow a few minutes later. Just act like you're really mad at me for being a snob, and I'll pretend I'm pissed at you for being all annoying. After we yell at each other, you can run out of the room to the bathroom and pretend you're crying, and Sheila can come after you. And Janie —"

"What?"

She held out her pinky. "I'm really glad you're my friend. Just don't forget that when I'm pretending to be a jerk."

I linked my pinky with hers and we shook. "Me too," I smiled.

I flushed the toilet – which was probably unnecessary, since nobody else was in the bathroom anyway - pretended to wash my hands and went back to class. Sure enough, Marcia had arrived and was standing in the back of the room, talking to Jessica. When I walked in, she looked up and gave me a little wave and a smile. Not really knowing how to respond – Marcia had never been nice to me before! – I kind of smiled back and went to sit down. Just when I had taken my English notebook and pencil case out of my bag, Kellie walked in.

She strode purposefully to her desk, ignoring me pointedly as she walked by. As she sat down, I turned around and shot her a dirty look.

"What?" Kellie said, facing me and looking annoyed. "What do you want?"

I took a deep breath and closed my eyes briefly, trying to put myself in an angry and insulted mindset. "What do I *want*?" My voice was shriller than I intended it to be.

"Yeah. What do you want? I get it. You think I'm a snob." Her face took on an actual sneer. "Well, maybe I am a snob. It's not *my* fault I have to rehearse every afternoon. You don't have to be such a *baby* about things. It's not like I'm ignoring you on purpose."

Hey, she was pretty good at this.

I stood up and walked towards her, vaguely aware that Alexis had come in and was standing by our desk, looking extremely uncomfortable. Out of the corner of my eye, I could also see Marcia watching us, a smug smile playing on her lips. She was clearly enjoying our little falling out. Sheila had just come in and was standing in the doorway, looking shocked, as if she had forgotten about our plan.

I gave Kellie what I hoped was another very dirty look. "You think you're so great just because you can sing! Well, you're the one being a huge *baby*. Believe me, my *dream* is for you to finally start ignoring me. You're such a jerk! And you're officially not invited to my sleepover party next week!" I walked towards Kellie and grabbed the pen she was holding. "And give me back my pen!" I turned and stormed out of the room, heading straight for the bathroom. I could feel everyone's eyes on me and just before the door swung shut I heard Kellie snort, "I wouldn't come to your stupid party if you paid me two million dollars!"

I locked myself in one of the stalls and stood next to the toilet seat, my heart pounding. I had forgotten to tell Sheila to come after me – I hoped she'd realize on her own that that was what she was supposed to do!

Two minutes later, the bathroom door opened and I could hear a knock on the stall door. "I'm in here," I said, trying to make my voice sound like I had been crying.

"Janie, it's me. And don't worry – the bathroom's empty."

I opened the stall door and smiled weakly at Sheila. "How was I?" I asked.

She grinned back at me. "You were most excellent. And I think it worked — just before I left, I saw MTS go up to Kellie and start talking to her." Sheila made a face. "That little jerk."

"She *did* seem happy to see us fighting," I said, splashing cold water on my face to make it look red and splotchy. "I guess we'll find out what she's up to soon."

******

After the bell rang, I walked slowly to my locker, still pretending to be sad. As I turned the dial on my combination lock, I felt a tap on my shoulder and turned around to see Jeremy standing behind me. He was taking huge bites out of a big Granny Smith apple and chewing loudly.

"Hey," he said. "You ok?"

"Um, yeah. I guess."

"That was crazy! I never saw you guys fight before. What's up with Kellie?"

I hesitated. I had figured on lying to Marcia, but I hadn't even thought about how we'd deal with everybody else. I guess I had no choice but to stick to my story.

"I don't know, she's just being incredibly stuck up!"

He nodded and took another bite of his apple. "I know what you mean. Maybe we were right about her to begin with."

I frowned. "What do you mean?"

"I mean, maybe she isn't as cool as everybody thinks she is. Ever since she was on Starbright, it's like everybody's under some kind of spell or something. Kids who didn't want to have anything to do with her when she first came to Middlestar are suddenly dying to be her best friend. But maybe there was a good reason nobody liked her in the beginning!"

I definitely didn't like the turn this conversation was taking. The last thing I needed was for our stupid pretend fight to make kids start hating Kellie again. But I couldn't defend her, or Jeremy would know I wasn't really mad. So I sniffed and just kind of shrugged noncommittally.

"Listen, I – uh – have to get to math now. I told Mrs. Santini I'd be a few minutes early today to go over the last test." Before Jeremy could say anything, I slammed my locker shut and raced down the hall toward the math room.

For the rest of the day, Kellie and I carefully ignored each other. It was a strange feeling - but the weirdest was lunchtime. A few minutes after Sheila and I grabbed our trays and sat down at our regular table, I saw Kellie come in with Marcia and sit down with her and Jessica at what used to be the cool table. Alexis came in a few minutes later, and even though I waved to her to come join us, she took her food and headed outside. Luckily, Jeremy, Calvin and Kevin didn't show up, and Sheila and I ended up eating alone. Somehow, even though I knew it wasn't for real, our table felt depressingly empty.

When the last bell finally rang, I zipped up my bag and went to wait for Sheila next to her locker. It was (finally!) time for her to come over to talk about Grandpa Charlie's key! I shoved my hands in my pockets and scanned the hall for Kellie, hoping to have a chance to talk to her, even for a few seconds. But when I finally saw her, she was surrounded by Marcia and Jessica, laughing at something I couldn't make out. I felt a twinge of uneasiness as she passed me without even looking in my direction.

"Snob!" I called out after her. But she didn't even turn around, and only Marcia looked back and sneered at me.

*****

An hour later, Sheila and I were sprawled out on the floor of the clubhouse, eating some of our leftover mint chocolate chip cookies and listening to the Glee Season 1 soundtrack. I inhaled deeply, closing my eyes and enjoying the warm breeze that wafted in from the yard. I am *definitely* a summer person. I even love how it smells.

I breathed out and looked over at Sheila, who was absentmindedly flipping through her English workbook. "Wait a minute," I asked, sitting up. "Do we have English homework for tomorrow? With all the drama this morning, I forgot to write it down."

"Huh?" Sheila looked up, confused. "Oh. No, I was just checking how many pages we have left until the end of the year."

"Why?"

"No reason." Sheila sat up too, snapping the book shut. "So, how do you think it's going? The whole Kellie and Marcia thing."

"Um.. I don't know. I guess it's going ok so far." Although truth be told, fighting with Kellie made me feel pretty lousy, and the whole business was starting to give me a bad feeling.

"Well, I guess it's time," Sheila said.

"Time for what?"

Sheila's my best friend, but she's not exactly the most patient person in the world. She rolled her eyes. "Time to start looking for your Grandpa's key. That's why I came over, remember?"

Grandpa Charlie's key. The one he had said would change everything.

******

There's so much stuff going on these days, sometimes I feel like I can barely keep track! It's funny – just a few months ago, my life was so incredibly *boring* that when my mom got me this diary, I thought it would be hard to come up with things to write about. It's not like I didn't have any friends – Sheila and I used to hang out and do stuff lots of times - but most days it was just school, homework, TV, computer time and not much else. And now, all of a sudden, things are happening so quickly, I barely have time to write at all! It's really lucky I got this diary when I did.

I picked up the brown, faded letter that lay on the rug and fingered it gingerly.

Technically, the letter was more than 25 years old – Grandpa Charlie had given it to me the very first time I used the medallion to travel back to 1985. I turned it over and looked at the last paragraph, as if reading it for what was probably the hundredth time would offer some clue as to its meaning: *When the time is right I have left you a key that will unlock more of the mysteries of the medallion. I put it under the loose floorboard of your mom's clubhouse, buried within the soil. But don't go looking for it until you're ready. It will change everything.*

Was I really ready for everything to change, even more than it already had?

I swallowed and glanced over at Sheila, who was looking at me expectantly. "I guess," I said in a small voice. Then I grinned, picking up a chair in the corner of the room and dragging it towards the clubhouse door. "Luckily there's only one floor board that's been loose for ages," I said. "We'd better hope it's the same one!"

******

Forty minutes later we were still digging, our clothes covered in dirt and the floor of the clubhouse a total mess. We didn't exactly have a real shovel, so we were using one of RJ's plastic beach toys. We were taking turns, but the ground was hard and it seemed like we were getting nowhere.

Then Sheila squealed with excitement. "Janie, look! I think I've hit something!"

I knelt down and peered into the hole, which was just about half a foot deep. "It's probably just another rock," I said.

"No, look!" Sheila scooped out a pile of dirt with her hands. Luckily, she had taken off the turquoise ring she'd started wearing pretty much every day lately. Her hands were filthy. "See – it's shiny."

I leaned over and peered in again. Sure enough, something plastic and silvery glinted in the light. My heart started to beat faster. "Wow, you're right!"

Sheila dug out a few more scoopfuls of dirt and then reached in and pulled out a small, shiny plastic box that was caked in mud. Hands trembling, she wiped it off and gave it to me.

"I – uh – I think maybe you should be the one to open it." For once, she actually sounded nervous.

I gulped, taking it from her, and held it in my hands. It was heavier than I had expected. I took a deep breath and looked over at Sheila. "Well, I guess it's now or…"

Before I could even finish my sentence, the box popped open and I jumped, startled. Inside was a long, heavy, old-fashioned looking key and a folded-up piece of paper. The key was silver and black, with a white number on it: 451. I put down the box and took out the paper, which oddly enough looked brand new. I unfolded it carefully and placed it on the rug between us. It was written in our secret language.

I picked up the note and started to decipher it. Sure enough, it said BEARER OF THE MEDALLION in big letters at the top of the page and was signed "Grandpa Charlie". When I finished copying it over in regular English, I cleared my throat and read aloud:

"BEARER OF THE MEDALLION

My dear, dear Janie,

So, I see you've decided to take the leap! Before you do, take a moment and think about whether you're really ready. As I told you, being Bearer of the Medallion is a very big responsibility. Once you use the key to unlock the secrets it protects, things will never be the same again.

And there is no going back."

I stopped reading and looked up at Sheila uncertainly. She was staring at me with a funny expression on her face, like she couldn't decide whether to be excited or terrified.

"He keeps saying that," I said, smiling weakly. A lame attempt to lighten the mood.

"Go on," Sheila said urgently, not taking her eyes off me.

I looked back down at the paper I was holding and kept on reading:

"If I remember correctly, you have chosen to share your knowledge with your friend Sheila. Remember: only one person can join you on your journey as Bearer of the Medallion. So make sure you have chosen wisely."

Sheila giggled. "Of course you chose wisely. You chose me! Doesn't get much wiser than that!"

I snorted and continued:

> *"The key you have found unlocks a vault at the United National Savings Bank on Crawley Street. The bank manager is a guy named Michael. They don't usually provide services to kids without an accompanying adult, but assuming you didn't wait too long to read this, he should be expecting you."*

"Expecting us?" Sheila broke in. "How could he be expecting us?"

"I don't know," I said softly.

> *"That's all you need to know for now. This has probably already taken you a long time to decipher! You'll understand more when you open the box.*
>
> *Hugs and kisses,*
>
> *Grandpa Charlie"*

I put the note down and picked up the key, dropping it into my jacket pocket and heading for the door. "Come on, Sheila," I said, a determined note in my voice. "It's time."

******

We got on our bikes and rode out to Crawley Street, stopping on the way to buy a blueberry muffin at Starbucks. My mom was out at a writer's workshop, so I sent her a Whatsapp from Sheila's phone, to let her know we were going for a ride. I'm usually allowed to go places that are in biking distance, as long as I let my parents know first – and as long as I come home on time. My mom gets so worried when I'm late, although I don't really get why. What does she think is gonna happen?

"Do you know where the bank is?" Sheila asked, slowing down as we passed Trader Joe's.

"I remember there being a bank right up here," I said, gesturing to the next corner. "Right after the pet shop."

Sure enough, there it was, right at the corner of Crawley and Montgomery Ave. United National Savings Bank. As we parked our bikes, I shuddered, suddenly feeling nervous. Going to the bank without a grownup was weird. My parents sometimes took me with them when they had to take out money or whatever, and once I remember waiting for my dad for what seemed like *forever*, exceedingly bored and counting backwards from a thousand to pass the time. Were we just supposed to walk up to this Michael character and introduce ourselves? And was he just going to let a couple of eleven-year-old girls open a vault, all by themselves?

"Well, here goes nothing," I muttered, pushing the door open. A burst of cold air rushed out and I shivered. "It's freezing in here!" I whispered to Sheila. I don't know why I whispered, it's not like it was the library or anything. It just seemed like the kind of place where you were supposed to be quiet.

We stepped inside and looked around. The bank was big and pretty fancy, with huge chandeliers and a design on the shiny, marble floor that reminded me of the Roman art we saw on our field trip to the ancient history museum. The walls were high, made of stone, and some of them seemed to have little inscriptions on them. I peered closely at the words engraved into the wall next to the entrance: "A person who never made a mistake never tried anything new – Albert Einstein".

How odd.

It was nearly six, and the bank was crowded. A long line of tired-looking grown-ups stood waiting for the tellers and a few people sat on fancy upholstered chairs reading magazines. For several minutes we stood there uncertainly, until Sheila pointed at a bowl of Jolly Rancher sucking candies on a large stand in the center of the room.

"Oh look!" She exclaimed, a bit too loudly. "I love those!" She started walking in the direction of the candy as several heads turned to stare at us. I could feel myself starting to blush. Leave it to Sheila to get sidetracked by *candy*.

"Shhh!" I tugged at Sheila's shirt and motioned for her to stop. "We didn't come here for that! We can't act like little kids if we want them to take us seriously!"

"Fine," Sheila muttered. "But I don't see what the big deal is."

Just then, something caught my eye and I almost had a heart attack. One of the inscriptions, carved out in huge block letters on the wall we were facing, had seemed at first to be in a foreign language. But as I stared at it, I realized I recognized one of the words: "**jki**" – or "the" in our secret language!

"Sh-Sheila," I stuttered, grabbing Sheila's arm and pointing dumbly at the inscription.

"What?" Sheila looked at the wall and back at me. "What is it?"

"It's – I mean.." I could barely speak. "The words on the wall over there. Don't you see?"

Sheila squinted in the direction I was pointing and wrinkled up her nose. "Janie, I don't have any idea what you're talking about!"

"The words over there! Don't you see? They're in our secret language!"

"They're what?!" Sheila had taken a sip from her water bottle and nearly spat it out on the floor.

"Look! I remember the word **jki**, from the translation I did this afternoon. It means **the**!"

"Holy guacamole," Sheila said under her breath. I don't know why we were so surprised. It's not like this was the first time something incredibly weird and unexpected had happened to us. I mean, what's a little inscription on the wall of a building compared to traveling through time to meet your mom when she's a little kid??

"It stinks that I don't have our letter key with me," I said, searching my pockets. "Do we have time to go back home and get it?"

Sheila pulled out her phone and looked at the time. "I don't know. It's already after six. If we go, we might not make it back before the bank closes. And anyhow, I'm not allowed to ride after dark."

I sighed. "Neither am I."

Then suddenly it hit me. "Wait! I don't have the letter key, but I do have Grandpa Charlie's letter and my translation. I'll bet we can use that to decipher the code."

I pulled out the letter and flattened it out on the stand in front of me. A few minutes later I smiled triumphantly. "Got it!"

"So what does it say?" Sheila was more impatient than ever.

"It says: The only reason for time is so that everything doesn't happen at once". A chill went through my body as Sheila and I looked at each other. This was creepy.

"What does that mean?" Sheila finally asked.

"I don't know," I said, rubbing my temples. I pulled out my tablet and opened the internet browser. "I guess I'll Google it."

Before I could finish typing in the inscription, I felt a hand on my shoulder, and turned around to see a man in a suit and tie standing behind me. He reached out to shake my hand. "You must be Janie," he said in a pleasant voice. "And you must be Sheila. I'm Michael Walleger. I believe you're here to see me?" He was tall and mostly bald, with just a bit of thinning brown hair and blue eyes that were sharp, but kind. He seemed to be about my dad's age.

"Um, yeah." I managed. I can be incredibly articulate when I'm nervous.

He gestured towards a small room in the corner, with glass windows. "Please come with me."

******

When we were seated in his office with tall cups of icy, sweet lemonade, the man leaned back in his chair and eyed us carefully. When he finally spoke he said, "Albert Einstein."

"Huh?" I said. Wow, I was going to get the Articulate Preteen Prize of the Month.

"Albert Einstein," he said again. "The quote on the wall. The only reason for time is so that everything doesn't happen at once. I think of all people, you girls probably know how true *that* is." He raised an eyebrow at us. "The inscription was a gift to the bank in 1933."

Sheila and I glanced at each other uneasily. 1933? And what was it with this bank and Albert Einstein? I struggled to get my voice back. "When, uh, when was the bank first built?" Great, Janie, way to a make a good first impression.

"Excellent question!" The man turned around and pointed to a plaque on the wall behind his desk. "1856. Almost 150 years ago."

"Amazing!" Sheila was shaking her head.

"Yes it is, isn't it," the man murmured. Then he turned to me. "So, Janie, you're really here. Your grandfather said you'd probably come before the summer, but we could never really be sure – "

"Wait," I broke in. "My grandfather? When did you speak to my grandfather? He's been dead -"

"Oh. Yes, well." He began straightening a pile of papers on his desk, avoiding my eyes and looking uncomfortable. "I'm not privy... Let's just say he paid us a little visit."

My heart skipped a beat. So Grandpa Charlie had taken a trip to the future! That must explain why the note we found with the key looked brand new – he must have added it recently!

I felt a pang of disappointment. Why hadn't he come to see me?

The man interrupted my thoughts. "The key," he was saying. "Do you have it?"

"Oh, yeah. Of course." I rummaged in my pocket and pulled out the long, shiny key.

He picked it up and twirled it around in his fingers. "Good. So there we have it." Standing up, he moved aside a large life-sized portrait of an elderly man to reveal a tall door with an enormous digital combination lock. I gulped as I read the code he punched in: 451451451. Then he reached out his hand and I gave him the key. "This vault hasn't been opened in over twenty-five years," he remarked, turning the key and pushing the door open. "And I must say – we've been waiting for you for a very, very long time."

******

195

Once inside, I was struck by the unremarkable nature of the room. It was about the size of a large walk-in closet and was covered on three sides by ceiling high, reddish brown mahogany bookshelves. In the middle of the room stood a small table and two folding chairs.

"Wow," I said under my breath, looking around. The shelves were filled with hundreds of small books, some of them as thin as comic books, and each shelf was marked with a different set of numbers.

"Wow is right," the man said. He gave a short whistle and then frowned. "Wait a minute. How is this —" He was pointing at the bottom shelf in the very corner of the room, the only one that still had space on it. "How can that be?"

"How can what be?" I squinted to get a closer look.

"That! Look at the numbers on the bottom shelf."

I bent over and read the markings aloud: "1995-2011. What does that mean?"

"It means that even though this vault hasn't been opened in more than 25 years, it contains very recent Histories. That really shouldn't be possible."

"Oh!" Sheila exclaimed. "You mean the numbers on the shelves are supposed to be dates?" She breathed in sharply. "Wow, so that means there are books here from -" her eyes scanned the shelves on the other side of the room and then widened. "4000 BC! Janie, look at this!"

I nodded numbly, at a loss for words. "Um, Mr. Walleger —"

"Please, call me Michael," he said, chuckling softly. "You don't know how long we've all been waiting for this moment, and what a relief it is to know that all of this," he gestured expansively, "has been successfully passed on."

I glanced around again, still dumbfounded. "Ok, uh, Michael. What is all this stuff? And what are we supposed to do with it?"

He chuckled again. "That much I don't know. I have been entrusted to ensure the safe transition of the materials to your possession. Beyond that — it is not my job to poke my nose where it is not welcome."

"But do you know what's in all these books?"

Michael looked shocked, as if I had asked him if he had three heads. "That is forbidden!" he said sharply. Then his voice softened. "Only the Bearer of the Medallion and her Companion are allowed to read the Histories. I may have no knowledge of their contents, nor am I permitted to ask unnecessary questions. I am simply to do my job. Which, it would seem, I have done. So there it is. I will leave you now and get back to the fascinating task of approving mortgages and arranging bank loans." He raised his eyebrows again and grinned. "Truly inspiring work, if I do say so myself."

"Wait, but —"

"Don't worry," he said as he opened the door to leave. "Be patient. Everything will become clear." He glanced at his watch and then reached into his pocket, taking out the key and leaning forward to give it to me. "The bank will be closing in fifteen minutes. Take this with you, and you can come back again tomorrow or whenever you need to. I'm here every day."

I swallowed hard as the door closed behind him with an ominous thud and glanced around the room. My eyes were drawn to the shelf in the bottom corner of the room, and I knelt down to take a closer look. The shelf had about fifteen little books on it, the last one lying face down. I picked it up and was startled to discover that while I expected it to be old and brittle — or at the very least covered in dust — it was a brand new Staples composition notebook. You know, one of those black and white hardcover notebooks you use for English class and stuff. On the cover it said "2011" in smudged red marker.

I opened it up to a random page, and my breath caught as I saw an entry marked "March 2011 – Janie returns home", and another one entitled "April 2011 – Janie uses medallion to help Kellie win Starbright".

I flipped ahead to the last page and nearly shrieked when I saw the heading: "August 12, 2011 – Janie takes first trip as Bearer of the Medallion". I snapped the book shut, my hands trembling and sank slowly down into one of the chairs in the center of the room. My legs felt like jelly and my heart was racing.

"What is it?" Sheila asked, sitting down next to me.

"These Histories aren't only about the past," I managed. "They're about the future too."

Sheila shivered and stared back at me, as pale as a ghost. For once in her life, she appeared to have been rendered speechless.

♥ May 10, 2011 ♥

Dear Diary,

As we left the vault last night, Michael handed us another note from Grandpa Charlie. It was also written in our secret language, and by the time I got home I was so exhausted, I just stuffed it under my mattress and went right to sleep. My eyes closed even before my head hit the pillow, and by nine o'clock I was out like a light. I slept so deeply that I barely heard my alarm clock this morning.

But the weird part was the incredibly creepy dream I had last night. I almost never have nightmares, but this one seemed so vivid, it felt like it was real. And when I finally did wake up, I had this awful sinking feeling in my stomach.

Sheila and I are riding our bikes to the bank, but instead we somehow end up at school. Only — it doesn't really look like our school: the building is old and run down, with cracks in the windows and stuff, and it's completely dark. I look at Sheila and swallow hard — something about the situation is definitely wrong, but I can't put my finger on it. So we park our bikes where we usually do and slowly walk inside. The hallways look even worse than the outside - with lots of dust, cobwebs and broken desks, and it seems like no one has been inside for ages. For some reason we're looking for the principal's office, and we can't find it — it isn't where it usually is. And then we see this huge sign with a big arrow on it, and Auditorium scrawled across it in shaky handwriting. I grasp Sheila's trembling hand, and suddenly it becomes clear — we don't need the principal's office, we need to be in the auditorium! And then, just as we start heading in that direction, Alexis appears — out of nowhere — sitting at a small table in the hallway and playing Solitaire with a deck of cards.

That's when the dream started becoming really spooky.

I call out to Alexis, to ask her what she's doing there, but she just keeps on dealing the cards and ignoring me. Finally, she looks up, and without a word shoves a card in my face. I gasp when I see what's on it – a picture of me, with the words Mean Girl written underneath! Then Sheila and I find the auditorium and go inside, and even though it's pitch dark we can see Marcia sitting inside at a desk, all alone. As we approach her, we can see she's crying. And she just keeps rocking back and forth and saying, "I can't take this test, I didn't study!"

I woke with a start and jumped out of bed, rushing over to turn on the light. My heart was pounding. Without even brushing my teeth or going to the bathroom, I ran downstairs as fast as I could and raced into the kitchen.

"Hi Janie!" my mom said, turning off the eggbeater as I came in. She looked at me quizzically.

"Um, hi." I tried not to show how out of breath I was as I slipped into a chair at the kitchen table. I'm too old to be scared of silly dreams, right? "Um, what are you making?"

"Gluten free pancakes," my mom answered, turning on the stove and adjusting the heat. She turned around to face me. "RJ's staying home today."

"Why?"

"Doctor's appointment. And since I have to do a bunch of errands this morning anyway, I thought I'd just take him with me." She glanced at the clock on the microwave. "I'd better go get him up."

The image of Marcia from my dream, sitting and crying in the auditorium flashed in my mind, and I flinched. And then, before I realized what I was saying, I heard myself ask in a small voice. "Mommy, can I come with you?"

My mom raised an eyebrow, surprised. "Why, honey? You have school today."

"I know. It's just – "

Now she looked concerned. "What? Is something wrong?"

A lot of my friends have to pretend they're sick when they want to stay home from school. I'm lucky – my parents have a very strict 'no lying' policy, but they also let us stay home sometimes just because we feel we need a break. They're big believers in what they call "mental health days." To be honest, I think my mom kind of regrets not having homeschooled us, and once in a while she even brings it up as a possibility. But most of the time I like school – I don't always love the work, but I like seeing my friends and all. I don't think I would like being home all the time.

"Uh, no, everything's fine." I avoided my mom's eyes. Being honest didn't mean I had to tell her *everything*, did it? And everything *was* fine, after all.

"Well, Janie," my mom was saying, "it's up to you. But I think you should go to school. You missed a bunch of days last month."

URGH! Isn't it annoying when parents tell you something's up to you but make it clear that there's really only one right choice? I seriously HATE that.

Just then, RJ ran into the kitchen and plopped down in the chair across from me. I rolled my eyes - he had his ear buds on. Ever since my dad gave him his old mp3 player, he's been walking around listening to stuff incessantly. He even goes to sleep with it, and my parents sneak in and turn it off after he's out for the night. And he doesn't even listen to music like a normal person – he's become obsessed with audiobooks and story podcasts.

I waved my hands in front of his face. "Hellooo, RJ." When he didn't answer me, I reached out and tickled him. He giggled and squirmed away, adjusting his earbuds and facing the wall.

"Mom," I called out. "RJ's wearing his mp3 at the table again."

"RJ!" my mom came back into the room and put a plate of pancakes in front of him. "Put those away for breakfast. And you -" she gestured towards me. "Mind your own business. RJ has enough parents without you."

RJ grinned at me and cackled, but didn't take out his earphones. "I paused it," he said.

"Nice try," my mom said. "Take them off." She picked up his plate and put it back on the counter, handing it back again only after he reluctantly pulled out his earbuds and gave them to her.

"Janie, what about you? Do you want some?" my mom pointed at the pancakes and smiled at me. "You should have a good breakfast."

"Nah. I mean – no thanks." I sighed, standing up and pouring myself a glass of orange juice. "I'm not so hungry. But I guess I'll go to school."

******

The day passed excruciatingly slowly. In second period, Kellie winked at me across the room as Mrs. Santini returned some English assignments we handed in ages ago. I winked back, but even though Marcia was sitting right in the front row, whispering something to Jessica and laughing, the image of her crying in my dream flashed in my mind again and my stomach clenched.

Sitting next to Alexis was really uncomfortable. Usually I love sharing a desk with her, but today it was like neither of us knew what to say to one another. She just bent over her notebooks, writing down everything the teacher said, and pretty much ignored me. I wanted to say something to her, but couldn't think of anything.

After third period, I practically bumped into her next to the water fountain. "Hi!" I said shyly, offering her a smile.

She smiled back, but just muttered "hi" and looked down at the floor. We had become such good friends lately, and now we could barely say two words to each other.

"Alexis, I – "

She looked up at me. "Janie, I'm sorry. I don't mean to be a jerk, it's just –" she paused. "I don't like what you're doing to Marcia. I know she's not the nicest person in the world sometimes, but she's been my friend for a long time…" her voice trailed off.

There was a long silence as I stood there uncomfortably, not saying anything.

"It's not too late to call it off, you know," Alexis finally said, bending over to take a drink of water. As she spoke, I imagined her shoving a card in my face and shook my head to banish the picture from my mind. She stood up and looked at me sadly, before turning around and walking off.

At lunch, I took my tray and sat with Sheila at our usual table. Even though it was pizza day – and I generally *love* pizza day – I wasn't really hungry. I just kind of sat there, pushing the overcooked cauliflower side around on my plate, and watching Kellie and Marcia across the room. They were sitting at the far table with Jessica, and seemed to be absorbed in conversation.

"So what do you think?" Sheila was saying. "Janie?"

"Huh?"

Sheila rolled her eyes at me. "Did you listen to anything I just said?"

I shrugged sheepishly. "I guess not, sorry. What were you talking about?"

"Well, I have to babysit for Gertie again this afternoon, so I thought maybe you could come over and we could make some more cookies. You know, practice for the contest."

"I guess," I nodded distractedly.

Sheila rolled her eyes again. "Janie, what is it?"

I looked at her and sighed. "I don't know. It's just – I had a really bad dream last night about Marcia and everything. And Alexis is really mad at us. I think maybe we should – "

"Janie, you're making way too big a deal about this. Think of it this way: if Marcia passes the test, she'll never see the inside of the fake diary. It's really up to her. And if she fails the test and tries to steal your diary – she deserves whatever she gets!"

"Yeah, but... Alexis keeps saying that Marcia acts so mean because she's really insecure. And she's the one who really knows her."

"Well, like I said. If she passes the test, there's nothing to worry about – she won't even know the difference." Sheila picked up her tray and stood up. "Come on, we're going to be late for math."

******

When school was finally over, we headed to Sheila's house. Gertie and her mom were already there.

"Oh hi, honey," Sheila's mom said, leaning over to give her a kiss. "Amy and I were just getting ready to leave. There's lasagna in the fridge, so you can warm it up in the microwave when you're ready to eat. And I got you the mint extract and chocolate chips you asked for." She indicated the counter next to the stove. "They're right over there."

"Thanks, Mom." Sheila reached over and tweaked Gertie's nose. "We'll be fine." Gertie giggled and jumped up and down. She was wearing purple overalls with a light green shirt underneath, and matching sandals. Her hair was carefully parted down the middle, and she had two little ponytails which were tied up with purple and white ribbons.

"I'm sure you will," Gertie's mom said, smiling at us. "You know, Gertie doesn't usually like staying with babysitters, but she's always happy to spend time with you, Sheila. She really likes you."

Sheila blushed. "Thanks, Aunt Amy."

Once the two moms had left, Sheila started taking out the cookie ingredients and spreading them out on the counter. She turned to Gertie. "So, kiddo, you want to help us? You can hold the mixer if you like."

Gertie nodded happily, pushing a chair over to the counter and climbing up on it. "I want to help!" she exclaimed.

Sheila and I grinned at each other. She was so cute!!

While Sheila and Gertie made the cookies, I mixed the ingredients for the royal icing, licking the powdered sugar off my fingers. Yum. We had decided to make Minion cookies for the contest, so I made yellow, black and white icing. I love the movie Despicable Me!

Once the cookies had cooled, we made a little decorating station on the kitchen table and gave Gertie a few cookies that she could decorate by herself. She pretty much made a mess, and by the time we were finished, she had yellow icing all over her face and even in her hair.

"Cookies!" she said gleefully, taking a big bite out of one of her gloppy creations. She picked up her doll and put a cookie near its mouth. "Dolly wants cookies too!"

Sheila reached over and gently took the doll from her hands. "Dolly can have cookies, but first we should let them dry so she doesn't get icing all over her."

Gertie giggled, cheerfully taking another bite. "We can give dolly a bath!" she said.

"I don't know about that," Sheila said in a sing-song voice. "But I know someone else who should probably get washed up." Sheila's one of the youngest babysitters I know, and she's really good with little kids. Somehow, when she babysits, she manages to be super patient- not usually her strong point - and she makes the kids laugh like crazy. Gertie happily took her hand and followed her into the bathroom, where she washed the icing out of her hair and changed her into a clean pair of shorts and a tee shirt.

A half an hour later Gertie was watching Nickelodeon in the living room, while Sheila and I cleaned the kitchen.

"Isn't Gertie adorable?" I asked, wiping the table with a Huggies diaper wipe. Sheila's parents still buy wipes, even though it's been years since they've had to change anybody's diaper. Her mother says they're very good for cleaning with.

"Yeah, she's cute," Sheila agreed. "But my Aunt Amy wasn't kidding about her hating babysitters. Ever since my aunt got sick, Gertie's been afraid to be away from her. And she acts out a lot. I overheard my aunt telling my mom that she even had to pick Gertie up a few times from preschool because she was hitting other kids."

"Gertie hitting other kids? I can't even imagine that," I said, surprised.

"Yeah, neither can I." She lowered her voice, glancing in the direction of the living room. "My aunt also said one babysitter quit after Gertie bit her."

"Bit her?? That's impossible." I tried to imagine sweet little Gertie biting someone, but I couldn't even conjure the picture in my mind.

"I know, right? But the truth is, the first time I babysat for her, it was kind of hard. She started crying that she wanted chocolate ice cream, and when I told her we didn't have any, she had the most humongous temper tantrum. Just like in the movies! She threw herself down on the ground and started pounding the floor with her fists and screeching her head off. She was making so much noise, I thought the neighbors were going to call the police or something."

I frowned, trying to picture little Gertie screaming and crying. "So what did you do?"

"Well, at first I got mad and kind of yelled at her to stop. But that just made things worse. She actually picked up a drawing I'd been working on all morning and threw it into the sink! I completely freaked out. And then – I don't know how it happened, but I suddenly got all quiet, like I was looking at the situation from outside, and I felt really calm. I started to imagine what was making Gertie so upset and it hit me that she must be scared being in a new place away from her mommy. Anyway, once I realized that, it was easy. I asked her if she wanted to call her mommy and say hello, and that did the trick. Well, that and reading Go, Dogs, Go about thirty times in a row." Sheila grinned. "Since then, it's been really easy to babysit for her."

I looked at Sheila admiringly. She could be stubborn, impatient and a little bit wacky – but she was one smart person.

I was quiet for several minutes as a thought formed in my mind. Then I said, "People can really act weird when they're scared. What if…" My voice trailed off.

"What if what?" Sheila picked up one of the eggbeaters and started licking it.

When I didn't answer, she shot me an exasperated look. "Don't tell me you're obsessing about this whole Marcia thing again! You are such a banana brain sometimes!" She handed me the other eggbeater. "Here, lick this."

I took it from her, just as a big glob of batter dripped off onto the floor. I bent down to wipe it up. "Well, if Alexis is right, and Marcia's mainly insecure, testing her will just make things worse. If she says she wants to be our friend, we should just be nice to her and invite her over or something. What's the worst that could happen?"

Sheila snorted. "The worst that could happen with Marcia? How much time do you have?"

I sniffed. "Well, I've changed my mind. I think we should give her a chance. And hey – if worst comes to worst, we can always go back in time and fix it!"

Sheila sighed and threw her eggbeater into the sink. "Well I guess there's no arguing with the Bearer of the Medallion."

She raised an eyebrow at me and I grinned, a feeling of relief washing over me. "Indeed."

******

When I got home, the house was quiet. RJ was sitting at the kitchen table eating a popsicle and leafing through a comic book, and my mom was hunched over her laptop in the dining room. A pot was boiling on the stove and I walked over, opening it and breathing in deeply.

"Wow, Mom, that smells really delicious!" I said, putting the cover back on and opening the refrigerator.

"Thanks." My mom looked up, surprised. "It's lentil soup. If you dare to taste it, I think you'll like it."

Normally I'd wrinkle up my nose and protest a weird food like lentil soup, but for some reason I was in a really, really good mood. "Sounds yummy." My mom beamed at me.

As soon as I got upstairs, I called Alexis and Kellie to fill them in on what Sheila and I had decided. Alexis was really happy. "I knew you'd come around!" she said when I told her the news.

Kellie was in the middle of a voice lesson, but a couple of hours later she called me back.

"That's great," Kellie said, when I told her I was planning to invite Marcia over. "It's funny – now that I've been spending all this time with her, I can see what Alexis is talking about. I don't think she's a bad person. I was starting to feel guilty about our trick," she admitted.

I sighed with relief. I had been worried Kellie would be mad at me for going back on our plan.

♥ May 11, 2011 ♥

Dear Diary,

This morning when I woke up, the first thing I did was feel under my mattress to make sure Grandpa Charlie's new note was still there. I sighed with relief – it was. Last night I dreamed that RJ snuck into my room during school yesterday and stole it! I don't know what's up with me and dreams lately, usually I don't even remember them.

The second thing I did was double check that I had put the food coloring in my backpack. Sheila was going to bring the rest of the ingredients. I smiled to myself as I got dressed – this was going to be an awesome day!

The baking contest was supposed to be during third and fourth periods, which meant no math and no science. And I was really glad Kellie and I were done with the whole fighting thing. The contest would be so much more fun with her and Alexis around.

I came down to breakfast whistling under my breath and patted RJ on the head. He was sitting at the table eating gluten free cornflakes one by one and drinking milk out of a sippy cup. Impulsively, I reached out and gave him a hug. He screwed up his face at me and squealed "Ew, gross!", wiggling away. I just grinned at him. He could be pretty cute sometimes.

"Why are you so chipper?" my mom looked pleased as I helped myself to a big bowl of Cheerios and milk. The other day I overheard her talking to my dad about how now that I'm becoming a preteen, I'm moodier than I used to be. Which I think is ridiculous. Just because I like to be alone sometimes, and not to tell my parents every little thing, doesn't mean I'm moody.

"No reason," I said, my mouth full of cereal.

The baking contest went really well. We ended up making regular chocolate chip cookies and using the mint extract in the royal icing. It was really yummy, and the Minions came out looking great. Alexis didn't enter the contest – she likes eating more than baking. And even though Kellie and I made a big show of making up, she was still Marcia's baking partner. They made brownies.

The best part is – Sheila and I won second place! Jeremy and Kenny won first place, with a salty-sweet pecan pie topped with vanilla ice cream. Marcia and Kellie didn't even get an honorable mention. To be honest, their brownies were kind of run-of-the-mill.

The second-place prize was a 10$ gift certificate to Absolutely Muffins. So we decided to pool our prizes and go there after school with the whole gang – Alexis, Kellie, Sheila, Calvin, Kenny, Jeremy and I. And we even invited Marcia and Jessica! I had an Allspice Apple Crumb Delight – which was awesome. Sheila had a gigantic corn muffin, but most of the other kids stuck with regular old chocolate chip.

Afterwards, I invited all the girls back to my house to watch How to Train Your Dragon. Jessica had to get a haircut, and Kellie had to go home and practice for Starbright (what else??) but Sheila, Alexis and Marcia came over. Inviting Marcia was kind of awkward, but she seemed really happy to come, and having Alexis around made it a bit less weird.

As I set up the movie in the living room, my mom came in and asked if anyone wanted a snack.

"Sure!" Sheila said. "Thanks, Mrs. Ray." Sheila comes over so often that she's practically a member of our family. So she's not embarrassed to ask for food or anything. Alexis, on the other hand, gets really shy around adults and just kind of shook her head and muttered "No, thanks." You won't believe this, but Marcia was also pretty shy.

A few minutes later, my mom brought in a huge bowl of popcorn and a plate of cut up apples, cucumbers and carrots. We pop our own fresh popcorn at home, on the stovetop. It actually comes out really good that way, and my mom says it's much healthier than the microwave kind.

"Wow, you're so lucky!" Marcia whispered at me after my mom left the room. "Your mom is so nice!"

"Um, thanks," I said. I wondered what she meant. I mean, I love my mom, but all she did was bring us a snack. Don't all moms do stuff like that?

About halfway through the movie, I noticed that Marcia was gone. "Where's Marcia?" I mouthed to Sheila.

"I don't know," she shrugged. "Maybe she went to the bathroom or something.

"Maybe." When several minutes had passed and Marcia still wasn't back, I paused the movie and stood up. "I'll be back in a second, guys," I said. "I just want to make sure she's ok."

I knocked on the bathroom door and there was no reply. How strange, I thought to myself. When I didn't find her after searching the rest of the downstairs, I went up to see if maybe she had decided to use the upstairs bathroom. And that's when I saw her, standing in my room and looking around.

"Marcia?" I said. "What are – "

"Oh my god!" she jumped as if she'd seen a ghost and then smiled sheepishly. "Sorry, Janie, you startled me!" She dropped something she had been holding and hurried towards the door.

"Um, it's ok." I looked at her quizzically. "What are you doing here?"

"Oh, nothing," she said nonchalantly. She gestured toward my wall. "I, um, just saw this poster here and I stopped to check it out. Sorry for going into your room without permission."

She was pointing at the fire safety poster I had gotten from the Forest Rangers after I helped put out the fire during our school trip (you remember that whole story, right?).

"Uh, No problem," I said, wondering vaguely why she'd be so interested in a boring old fire safety poster. Even I only hung it in my room because I got it as a prize.

We went back down to finish the movie, but my mind kept wandering to everything that's been happening. If you had told me just a few weeks ago that I would be traveling through time and exploring old bank vaults – or even that I would be friends with Marcia the Snob – I would have said you were stark raving mad.

After the movie, we sat around on the living room floor eating the rest of the popcorn and leftover cucumber slices. We were quiet, but the silence wasn't an awkward one. Finally Marcia turned to me. "Janie, I'm really sorry for being such a jerk and calling you Janie the Frizz and stuff. I actually really like your hair. Mine is so – boring. I'm really glad we're friends now."

"Me too!" I said, feeling magnanimous. I looked at Alexis, who had a big smile on her face. Wow, Alexis had been totally right. It was lucky we hadn't gone through with the whole testing thing. I guess people really just want other people to be nice to them and to understand them – just like Gertie.

******

After Alexis and Marcia left, Sheila and I went upstairs and finally read

Grandpa Charlie's new letter:

Dear Janie,

This is the last letter for now. If you've gotten it from Michael, you must have been at the bank and seen the inside of the vault. It's incredible, isn't it!

First order of business: I guess you've figured out by now that I eventually did get the medallion back from Ancient Egypt. Otherwise, how could I have left it for you to find in the future?

As I've told you, the Medallion has been passed down for centuries from grandparent to grandchild, and the Bearer carries great responsibility. It's time I told you more about what that responsibility entails.

Since the dawn of time, there have been those who seek to rule over other human beings. When misfortune strikes, they take advantage of the opportunity to wrest control and increase their power. The job of the Bearer of the Medallion is to maintain constant vigilance — to watch over history, and with minimal interference help prevent disasters.

Like I said, it is extremely dangerous to meddle in the past or to try and engineer the future. But there are moments in time when small, miniscule interventions can help avert major catastrophes. And it is at these moments when the Bearers must act and must record their deeds. It is for this reason that the Bearers are sometimes referred to as Historians. And as time goes on, you should read the Histories contained in the vault. Learning them will help you become adept at identifying the pivotal moments of history that require your intervention.

Janie, I know this isn't easy. And I know you must be asking yourself whether you're really up to the task. It is natural to doubt yourself. But I am confident you will succeed. You have everything it takes.

One last note — Don't ask Michael too many questions. He really doesn't know very much. He's part of the Outer Circle, a group that has existed for centuries and is committed to supporting the Bearers while remaining ignorant of the details. Michael is a good man, and you can rely on him in times of trouble. But he doesn't — and mustn't — know the full story.

I love you Janie, and I'm supremely proud of you.

Hugs,

Grandpa Charlie

For once, Sheila didn't interrupt me. And when I finished reading, we just sat there, our mouths hanging open, and stared at each other for what seemed like a really, really long time.

♥ May 12, 2011 ♥

Dear Diary,

O. M. G.

I think I'm going to faint, and my hand is shaking so badly, I don't think I can write more than a couple of sentences.

The medallion. IT'S GONE!!!!!!! I have to go look for it RIGHT NOW.

TO BE CONTINUED….

Continue the adventures of Janie Ray with Adventures 6 and 7, now available as a single paperback!

Turn the page for a free excerpt from book 6 of The Diary of Janie Ray, The Case of the Missing Medallion!

♥ May 13, 2011 ♥

You know how sometimes, when something bad happens, you wake up in the morning and it takes you a few seconds to remember that something's wrong?

Well, that's what happened to me this morning. For the first blissful moments after I opened my eyes, I looked out the window and sighed contentedly. The sun was shining, the birds were chirping, and a warm and peaceful feeling settled over me.

Then it hit me like a punch in the stomach, and I sat up abruptly, feeling the blood drain from my face.

The medallion was missing!!

I had stayed up until after midnight, searching every corner of my room and the clubhouse. I even emptied my desk drawers, dumping the contents on the floor and combing through them, and looked through all the pockets of my dirty laundry. It was really gone.

I jumped out of bed and changed into jeans and a tee shirt, quickly brushing my teeth and racing downstairs. I'm very picky about brushing my teeth – I hate having bad breath, and I can't stand the way my mouth feels in the morning before I brush. If there's ever a zombie apocalypse, I'll probably be the girl who gets eaten because she can't run away before making a stop in the bathroom!

"Hi, Janie!" my mom called out cheerfully when she saw me.

"Where's RJ?" I asked, so lost in my thoughts that I didn't even acknowledge her. If the medallion wasn't in my room, RJ's room was the next place I'd look. He's always peeking in through my door, and I know he's dying to get his little hands on my stuff!

"Hi Mom," my mom answered, raising an eyebrow at me. "I'm so glad to see you, Mom! Good morning, Mom!" My mom has a thing about polite greetings. If I come into the house and forget to say hi or whatever, she gets really annoyed.

I went over and gave her a quick hug. "Sorry, Mom. It's just -" My voice broke and I felt the sobs coming on.

"Janie, what is it?" She turned around to face me, a worried look on her face.

"My medallion! I lost it!"

My mom frowned. "What medallion, honey?"

I sniffed and took a deep breath, trying to stop myself from crying. *Janie, get a grip*, I thought. *Becoming hysterical is going to get you nowhere.* I steadied my voice. "The one I found in Florida, when I was seven!"

My mom gave me a puzzled look. Obviously, she had no idea what I was talking about, and she was probably thinking it was pretty strange for an eleven year old to be crying over some old souvenir!

She patted my head. "Don't worry, Janie, I'm sure it's here somewhere! Close your eyes and think back where you had it last. That usually works a lot better than just looking in random places." My mom should know – she's *forever* losing stuff, especially her keys. Once she left her wallet in the grocery store, and we spent all day looking for it! Finally, after she gave up and cancelled all her credit cards, somebody called from the store and said she could come pick it up. "That's Murphy's Law," she had said, shaking her head. At first I thought Murphy's Law was some kind of rule about returning things that are lost, but it turns out that's just an expression grown-ups use when things go wrong, like someone calling to return your wallet right *after* you cancelled your credit cards. Personally, I think if you're going to lose your wallet, you shouldn't complain if someone returns it, even if it takes a few hours!

"I looked everywhere, even in my hamper! I want to look in RJ's room. I'll bet he took it."

"I did not!" I hadn't even noticed RJ, sitting right there at the table in his pajamas, eating gluten free toast. He looked as indignant as someone can be with Nutella all over their face. "And you can't go into my room, anyway, remember?"

I sighed. I never told you about the family meeting we had a couple of weeks ago. It was after I complained to my mom for the seventeen millionth time about RJ coming into my room and messing up my stuff. My parents are big on having family meetings to Talk About Our Problems. It wasn't such a big deal, but the bottom line is, we made a rule that RJ and I can't go into each other's rooms without permission. Which is a great idea, in theory. Or rather – it would be, if RJ ever remembered it when he wanted to go into *my* room.

"RJ," I said calmly, "I lost something very important, and I need to look for it. Can I please go into your room?"

RJ shook his head smugly. "Nope. Just like you didn't let me in yesterday."

I clenched my fists, trying not to show how mad I was. "I know I didn't, I'm sorry – next time I'll let you!"

He looked up at me eagerly. "Promise?" He had such a hopeful expression on his face that I felt like a real jerk. The little guy really looks up to me, even if he is a pain most of the time.

I reached out and tweaked his nose. "Promise."

"Ok, you can go in. But I didn't take it!" He took a big bite out of his toast, waited a few seconds and opened his mouth so I could see the chewed up food.

"Gross!" I shrieked. But my expression softened. "I don't think you took it on purpose," I said. "But I just have to make sure it isn't in there."

******

I searched RJ's room for almost an hour before I had to leave for school. I didn't find the medallion, but I *did* find a Barbie that's been missing for almost a year and one of my favorite bracelets! RJ's lucky I'm way too upset about the medallion right now to care about other stuff.

I walked to school slowly, the knot that had formed in the pit of my stomach growing larger. This was nothing short of a disaster. Leave it to me to be the first Bearer of the Medallion to actually lose the darn thing! I couldn't even begin to imagine what the implications of this might be.

I didn't *want* to imagine.

I tried to think back to the last time I had used the medallion, going over and over the events in my mind. It was when we had gone to see Never Say Never, and I went back in time to fix the whole being-late-and-lying-to-my-parents fiasco. After that, I had decided to hide it in my closet and not use it again, until I figured out what I was *supposed* to do with it. And I'm 100% sure I never took it out after that! So it's not like I could have left it somewhere or anything.

When I got to school, Sheila was standing by the blackboard, talking to

Calvin. She was giggling at something, throwing her head back and looking very interested in what he was saying. I shook my head. Did she even know how ridiculous she looked? If she was trying to hide the fact that she had a MASSIVE crush on Calvin, she wasn't doing a very good job.

"Sorry, Calvin," I said, smiling apologetically. "I need to borrow Sheila for a minute." I grabbed her arm and dragged her into the bathroom.

"What the heck was that all about?" Sheila sputtered, straightening her shirt and looking at me like I had fallen from Mars. Ever since Calvin started hanging out with us, Sheila's been kind of dressing up for school. Like blow-drying her hair in the morning and wearing nicer shirts and stuff. Which, if you ask me, is pretty weird. I have to admit, Calvin's probably the cutest guy in our grade, but she acts all silly every time she talks to him, and it's really starting to get on my nerves.

I looked around to make sure the bathroom was empty. "The medallion!" I whispered loudly. "It's gone!"

"What do you mean, it's gone?" Sheila whispered back. Then she spoke in a regular voice. "And why are you whispering? Nobody's in here."

She had a point.

"I mean, it's gone! It isn't in my closet, and I've looked *everywhere* in my room and in the clubhouse. It's not there!"

Her eyes widened, and she just kind of stood there, looking at me. "Oh, no," she finally said.

"Oh no, indeed." I shook my head.

******

Somehow we made it through the morning, and at lunch we found a table in the far corner of the cafeteria. Kellie was home preparing for the Starbright Showdown – it's tomorrow, remember!?? And Alexis had a dentist's appointment. Which was lucky, because we couldn't talk about the medallion in front of them.

"We have to think about this logically," Sheila was saying. She twirled spaghetti around on her fork before taking a small bite and making a face. "Ugh. You know, the fact that they can mess up something as simple as spaghetti and meatballs is kind of a feat of nature, isn't it."

Leave it to Sheila to think about food at a time like this. "Actually, what's a feat of nature is that you can think about spaghetti when the world is coming to an end!"

"Sorry." She put her fork down. "Well, except for me and your family, who's been in your room recently?"

"Nobody -" I started to say, and then I stopped. Well, Kellie and Alexis had been there, but I couldn't imagine they would have taken anything. And -

"Oh, hi Marcia!" Sheila interrupted my thoughts.

And Marcia. Of course.

"Hi Sheila! Hi Janie!" Marcia was balancing her tray with one hand and waving to us with the other. She sat down across from Sheila and gave us a huge smile. "Mind if I sit with you guys? I had classroom duty, so I haven't even started eating yet!"

Sheila and I looked at each other. Just a couple of days ago, the idea of Marcia – A.K.A MTS or Marcia the Snob – eating lunch with us was pretty much unthinkable. She was queen of the "in crowd" and most definitely NOT my friend. She was the one who made up the whole "Janie the Frizz" business, and she never missed an opportunity to call Kellie "Kellie

Smelly". If we had asked to eat lunch with her and her crew of princesses, they probably would have laughed us out the cafeteria.

But ever since Kellie was on Starbright, Marcia's been trying really hard to become our friend. I'm still not sure I trust her, but Alexis – who's been friends with Marcia since they were little – wants us to give her a chance.

A couple of days ago MTS even came over to my house! And – you guessed it - she's the other person who was in my room. But she was only there for a few seconds. And I really don't think she took the medallion. First of all – when I came in, I saw her standing there and staring at the fire safety poster I got during our class trip. She wasn't rummaging through my closet or anything, and she didn't look the least bit suspicious! And second of all – she's trying really hard to get us to like her right now. Why would she risk losing all her new friends just to take some old medallion?

"Sure," I said, moving my tray back to make room for Marcia's. "Have a seat. We were just trying to figure out how the cafeteria could ruin something as basic as spaghetti." I took a bite. Wow, Sheila was right – it was rubbery *and* mushy. Which if you think about it, is quite an accomplishment. Yuck.

"Yeah, I know." Marcia started picking at the soggy green stuff that was supposed to be salad. "So!" she said brightly, changing the subject. "What are you guys doing this summer? My family's going to Italy for two weeks! And after that, I'm going to sleepaway camp for a whole month!" She brushed a few strands of hair out of her eyes.

I studied her. She was wearing a yellow short-sleeved shirt, a silver and black necklace that looked very exotic, and designer jeans. And somehow, even though it was only May, she was already tanned. It figured she'd have a completely fabulous summer planned.

"Um, I actually don't have any plans yet." I've been going to horseback riding camp since I was nine, but I told my parents I'm definitely not going back this year. The counselors are horrible. And the other kids all know each other from school. I love horses, but not enough to spend all day with kids who barely talk to me. Plus, the camp is very disorganized. Once we went on a three-hour ride and the counselors forgot to bring water! When we said we were thirsty, they told us to drink our spit. Which, besides being incredibly gross, doesn't actually make you less thirsty. And they acted like it was our fault! My parents called the camp director to complain, but I doubt it made much of a difference. I'm thinking maybe tennis camp. Or creative writing camp, if I can convince one of my friends to come with me!

Marcia nodded, and I could tell she was making a big effort not to look smug. She looked at Sheila. "What about you?"

"I'm going to my grandparents' house for a couple of weeks, and then I don't know."

"Oh," Marcia said. "Well, maybe we can all find a day to get together when I get back from Italy! I'm leaving the day after school ends. We'll be in Rome for a whole week, and then we're going to a horse farm in the north!"

"Wow," Sheila said wistfully. "That's awesome. I'm so jealous."

"Yeah," I said, raising an eyebrow at her. "We never go *anywhere*."

******

After school, Sheila came over so we could make a game plan. We *have* to find the medallion before tomorrow night! We all got tickets to go see Kellie in the Starbright Showdown, and I don't see how I'll be able to concentrate on the show if the medallion is still missing!

If you want to hear about how I used the medallion to help Kellie get on

Starbright, I wrote all about that whole business in earlier parts of the diary – so check it out, if you're interested. When she first came to Middlestar Elementary, Kellie was the most unpopular kid in our class, and everyone made fun of her. But that feels like ancient history. She has the best singing voice I ever heard, and if she wins tomorrow, she may be able to make her own album with a real production company!

"So where else can we look?" Sheila asked, lying back on my bed. "Are you sure it's not in your closet?" She gestured to the mess that was spilling out onto the floor. "It's not exactly the easiest place to find things."

"Yes, I'm sure. But I guess it can't hurt to look one more time."

Just as we finished dumping all my clothes out onto the floor, there was a knock on the door, and my mom peeked in.

"Hi girls, I thought maybe you'd want -" She stopped and stared at the huge mess on the floor. "What are you guys doing?"

"Oh, we're just -"

"We're sorting through Janie's clothes for the summer," Sheila interjected.

"Well, that's a very good idea!" my mom nodded approvingly. She handed us a plate of veggies. "I thought maybe you guys would want a snack. I have to do an errand, and RJ's coming with me. Oh – and if you're already sorting your clothes, maybe you could organize your closet while you're at it. It's always such a mess!"

Sheila stifled a giggle and I smiled. Ever since our little trip back to 1985, it's been hard to take my mom's pronouncements about my slovenliness quite as seriously. And I'll bet you know what I'm about to say: If you want to find out more about *that*, you can read earlier parts of my diary…

As we folded the last couple of shirts and put them back on the shelf, I let out a disheartened sigh. Obviously, searching the same places over and over again would get us nowhere.

"What about your desk?" Sheila asked.

"Nah, I dumped everything out last night," I shook my head. "There really isn't any point in doing it again."

"Well," Sheila said, ignoring me and opening my top drawer. "Sometimes it helps for someone else to look. Remember when I lost my necklace?"

A few months ago, Sheila went bananas when she couldn't find this genuine gold necklace she got from her grandmother when she was born. She didn't talk about anything else for almost a week. She thought she had looked everywhere, but finally her mom went through her dresser, and there it was, right between two pairs of shorts.

"Well, that's different," I said, closing the drawer. "I'm telling you, it isn't there!"

Sheila snorted and leaned back on the bed. "Fine, have it your way." Then, out of nowhere, she jumped up and shrieked. "I've got it!"

"What?!" I was getting annoyed.

"Well, remember the letters you got from your older self? Maybe you should write yourself a letter and ask for help! I'll bet Prof. Janie Ray will be able to tell you just where to find the medallion!"

I bit my fingernail, considering what she said. I had to admit, that was a pretty good idea. "Ok," I said slowly, sitting down at my desk and taking out a pen and paper. "Let's write a draft, and then I'll translate it into our secret language."

You already know what I'm going to say, so I won't bother. Yup, earlier parts of the diary. Plus, I've pasted our secret language into the back of the diary, so that I won't lose it. So you can look back there if you have no idea what I'm talking about.

I quickly finished the note and read it to Sheila.

Dear Prof. Janie Ray,

Hi, it's me again. Or rather, you. I have a huge problem. I can't find the medallion! I hope you remember when this happened, so that you can tell me where to look. I'm desperate!

Love,

Janie

"Ok," Sheila said, when I had finished copying it over in our secret code. "Let's hide it in your closet, where we put the other ones. Hopefully, she'll answer right away, like she did last time!"

I folded the note and stuffed it into the little crevice at the back of my closet. The last time I'd communicated with my older self, her answers had appeared almost instantaneously under the pillow on my bed. I guess she could just use the medallion to travel back to the exact right moment and leave them for me.

After a few tense seconds passed, I got up and felt around under my pillow.

"Anything there?" Sheila's voice was stiff.

"Nope." I sat down on my bed and waited, checking every few seconds to see whether anything had arrived.

"Maybe she's just busy," Sheila offered, sounding uncertain.

"I don't think so," I frowned. "Even if it takes her years to write back, she can still travel back to the exact right time to give us the answer. From our point of view, it should still be instantaneous."

"Right…" Sheila's voice trailed off. Then she reached again for my desk drawer. "What about the key you got from your Grandpa? The one we used to open the vault at the bank?"

My heart started racing and I felt another wave of panic coming on. "What about it? It should be right in here." I pushed in front of her and started frantically rummaging through the top desk drawer. I had been keeping the key in my desk, but I hadn't thought to notice whether it was there when I searched through it the night before. "Come on, it's got to - Oh, thank goodness, here it is." I grabbed the key and held onto it, slowing letting out a sigh of relief. My heart was still pounding. If the key had gone missing too, we'd really be in trouble.

As I started closing the drawer, Sheila stuck her hand in. "Wait, what's that?" She pulled out three pink notes that had been under the key.

"Those are the old notes from my older self, why?"

"Well, look at them!" Sheila turned around and shoved them in my face.

I turned the notes over in my hand, my mouth hanging open. They were there, but they looked like Swiss cheese, like a little kid had attacked them with a hole puncher. I could barely even see the words.

My first thought was – RJ! I can't believe that little brat came into my room *again* and messed up my stuff!!

But then I remembered – our hole puncher has been broken for ages. I've been bugging my mom to get a new one, but she keeps forgetting. Plus – the notes were just where I left them, and it really didn't look like anyone had touched them. I highly doubted RJ would come into my room, punch holes into pieces of paper, and then just put them back exactly where he had found them. That really didn't make sense.

Something was happening, and I needed to find out what - before things got completely out of control.

******

Made in the USA
Middletown, DE
03 March 2020